ECKOspace 6

by Jim Marcus

December, 2024

This book is set in Lato Regular 9/13
Titles in Lato Heavy 16/20

Cover:
Veda Ecko
by Jim Marcus 2024

ISBN 979-8-9917282-8-7

For all the people i still carry with me.

■ ┃ PULSEBLACK ┃ ┃

"What the mind doesn't understand,

it worships or fears."

-Alice Walker

-16 Days

It starts, like it always does, with me with this big fruity drink in my hand, laying down on one of those reclining pool chairs. I take a big swig and the sun reflects off pretty much everything so I close my eyes and slide that giant floppy white hat over my eyes that Kal bought me in Tulum.

And then the drink slips out of my hand, which is number one. That happens, making me sit up. Then there's some sort of alarm. In my brain, I'm thinking, "An alarm for a spilled drink? That's excessive." But that's number two. Then a bunch of noise, people running around. There's a scream.

And that's three. That wakes me up. I get up and I sort of run in that direction, but there are so many people. This is a resort. It's Mexico. It's just full of people, right? I hear it again from the pool. So I push through to get to the pool.

This is like pool number six at this place. It's a little smaller and it really has no shallow area. It's one of those lap pools, longish. But it's still fairly wide. People are freaking out because something caused the poly enclosure to start to slide close. It's closing slowly, but it's not, you know? It's closing the way zombies advance, slowly but unstoppably, inexorably. People are trying to keep it open. They can't.

Most people in the pool got out. But there is a girl in the far end, maybe twenty five. She could be younger. Honestly I can't tell people's ages anymore. But she was underwater. She didn't know. People are banging on the poly surface and she looks up and panics. You can tell she let the air out that she was holding and now there is a transparent ceiling over the pool that is preventing her from getting out.

She can't breathe.

I try to get to the side of the pool. There seems to be no one here who works here. It's just full of people, like all of earth is now. Just people everywhere. And they won't move fast enough.

I finally get to the side of the pool. I can't hold back the poly pool covering. I know there are mechanics that are supposed to stop this from happening but they seem to have malfunctioned. It's broken. And it won't stop.

The girl is swimming to the open end but you can tell she won't make it. I'm holding it, trying desperately to stop it but it just won't stop. I consider getting in the pool and blocking it but the water is nine feet deep throughout. It will either cut me in half or I'd drown. If there was a chance, I'd do it.

But there is no chance.

The screaming goes on. I'm doing it, too. There is another girl. Her friend? She's banging on the top of the pool covering, trying to break it, I guess. The girl swimming is running out of air.

Her eyes close. She breathes in water. She starts coughing, throwing up, as her body tries to breathe the water. Her black hair swarms around her like a living web I can't do anything and so I do the cowardly thing.

I wipe blood from a cut on my inside thigh. I look away.

And so do a lot of people. A man comes running from the restaurant area and starts shooting at the transparent covering as the girl twitches and dies.

The bullets ricochet and the other woman is shot in the arm. The shots stop. Eventually security comes and uses some odd key to open it, but it's too late. They fish her out.

She's dead. I put my head down and get back to my chair. Someone else is in it. So I go to the bar and stand there. It feels empty. There are literally thousands of people, everywhere I look. But not the ones I need. I look for Dae or Kal and I can't find them, either. My breathing starts to slow.

I go back to my room.

On the way some woman tells her husband that it's a horrible thing, but maybe it's for the best. There needs to be fewer people. And if you aren't smart enough to get out of the pool, maybe that's on you. I want to scream in her face, but there is no point.

In my dream, the girls are asleep in the room. I slide into bed with Dae and try to sleep but I keep seeing that girl.

We leave the resort two days later but we should have left right away.

There was no point. But that was the dream.

This time, though, I wake up next to Dae with the warm whir of the ship all around us. I feel the scar on the inside of my thigh from the pool.

I pull her close and pretend to be asleep.

"Hey, Zoo."

She knows I'm awake. Dae was a light sleeper.

"Are you coming for this call?"

I sigh. "Nope. I'm staying right here for a little longer. You go if you want. I don't have anyone to say goodbye to who isn't already bugging me on this ship."

"Fair. It's sixteen days. You good with that?"

"Am I ok with earthlings not telling me what to do for sixteen days? I will cope."

"Oh, the big bad earthlings."

"You know", I said to her. "A couple hundred years ago, NASA was going to send up a ship of all women."

"Oh, yeah?"

"Yeah, they were afraid the astronauts would have sex. So they solved that problem. Nipped it in the bud."

"That seems like a really great solution." She kissed me softly with her pretty pinkish brown lips.

"Well, you know, they were rocket scientists." I kissed her back, holding her arms over her head.

"They really were. " She put her legs around me and pulled me in.

"Yeah, do that."

"You want me to keep doing this?" she laughed.

"You don't need to do this call, do you?"

"I'm just the navigator. As long as the ship is heading forward, no one needs to interact with me."

"Forward, huh?" I climbed on top of her.

"Mostly. At least that's what I learned in navigator school."

"Fascinating. I'll remember that shit. Forward."

Just then, there was a buzz and Roja's Voice rang out from the comscreen. It was warm and thick and burly, just like him. It resonated.

"Captain, are you coming to this call?"

Dae and I both yelled out, "No."

"Go away."

I threw a pillow at the screen. "Fuck off."

He laughed. "That was fucking rude. Should I tell them that the captain's getting laid and can't be bothered?"

"And that they suck and they'll suck just as much in sixteen days."

"Aye Aye, you little Fucktoy."

"Captain Fucktoy, asshole."

Roja laughed. I was willing to bet twenty bucks that he was skipping the call, too. The way this trip worked, due to the method of travel, we were going to be unable to contact Earth for the next 16 days. This last call was just to catch them up on our location, leaving the solar system. Honestly, who cares. They're too far away to do anything if we were experiencing any problems. And once we reached Proxima Centauri B we'd be in touch the whole time.

They could do without us for two weeks or so.

So I sank into my girlfriend and enjoyed the morning.

Roja was in the Den when we got there. The black woman with the braids who was always smiling and ready to break out dancing was Kalista. She'd been my friend for over twenty years, longer than anyone else on the ship, but not by much. She was taller than me by a few inches but Roja had us both by over a foot. I slapped him on the back.

"So how did that go?"

"It was great. We're on schedule. I told them we'd be at Centuri B asap and it would be about 20 more years before we could wage sweet sweet war on Earth"

"And that went over?..."

"Badly."

Kalista Jumped in, "The president is very proud of us, though. We hear."

"That's cool. Maybe I should have voted for him"

I grabbed some eggs from the bowl in the middle of the table.

"Kal, Do you remember Isla Mujeres?"

"I remember Tulum. Cancun?"

"Jesus, how much fucking vacationing do you people do?" Roja got seconds on breakfast. We tried to talk over the music in the galley.

"Bitch, we're still on vacation." Dae high fived me. The quiet little Korean Navigator I had started dating three years ago on my last year-long mission was gone, replaced by this bigger than life Bratz doll. She seemed so much more comfortable and that made me happy.

"The pool. That girl?"

"I was drunk for that whole trip. Also, for a place called Isla Mujeres, there were a fuckton of men. So..."

Dae spoke up, "I remember because you told me. The girl got trapped under a pool cover and died. I think I slept through it."

"That's not supposed to happen," added Roja. "They stop, right?"

"Usually. Just not this time. I just had a dream about it again, is all."

Dae took a bite from her plate, "I'm trying to convince her to dream about all this," She made a motion at her body.

"That would not have malfunctioned on my watch, just saying," Roja beamed. He stuffed his face.

Kalista seconded, "Yeah, after he upgraded my bathroom to a bidet I'm basically honor bound to agree with that."

"And that little bribe is going to pay off."

Marin came in "He made my bed vibrate." Marin was a quiet man who was born in Brazil and had graduated college at fourteen with a pHd in biology. Roja had taken him under his wing immediately.

Kalista was curious, "You can do that?"

Roja looked across at her, "We're on a ship in a bubble moving at one hundred times the speed of light. Half of what I do here is making things NOT vibrate."

"I'm kind of amazed we do any work at all here sometimes," I thought out loud.

"On that note, I wanted to show you something, Captain." Marin pulled out a tablet. Part of me wished people could just call me Zedi and we could just be equals. I know that wasn't how it worked.

"What is this?"

"It's an anomalous life reading. I'm 99% sure it's a clump of cells containing an active virus or something, but it's in the quad area."

"That sounds ominous."

"Well, it shouldn't. We're all mostly virus."

"I'm mostly Bacon and bad thoughts," Roja quipped back.

"Our introns- junk DNA. They are partially viruses. Things our ancestors were exposed to. Almost none are dangerous.

"So, we need to figure out what that clump of cells is?"

"Or not. If it gets bigger, sure, we may want to. Otherwise, it's probably no big deal."

"Ok. When Lyra gets here, why don't you guys check it out. Wear gloves. Ick."

"Roger that."

"Where is Lyra?" The petite redhead who served as medical officer was, along with Marin, the one I knew the least about. This was their first mission with us and it was a big one.

A one way one.

We were headed about four point two light years away to the second planet of Proxima Centauri, a planet that looked to be able to support life. Our job was to establish the colony that the larger ships would eventually populate. The generation class ships would take their time, though. The first one had been sent out about twenty years ago and it would arrive about a year after we did. We would meet them with all the tools needed to survive and thrive, two decades more advanced than they were. Compared to a Generation class ship, the Veda ECKO 6 was tiny.

But it was very fast. And this would be the farthest a ship like this had ever gone.

"Ok, you are all really bad people," Lyra stepped into the dining area and grabbed a banana. "I just talked to the president all by myself."

"Are you in charge now?" That would be kind of a relief. I could play video games for the next year.

"Ha. I don't want any of your jobs. I barely want mine. I've seen you all naked. That's my trauma to live with."

Roja looked up,"Even if she weren't my doctor, she would have seen me."

"I was curious," she sat down.

Marin showed her the tablet, "We're going to check this out in the quad."

"That's weird. Did someone throw up there?"

"I thought that, too, but that doesn't really track. It's probably been here since takeoff and we're just seeing it now.

She held up the banana, "I'll finish this and meet you."

I stood up, "ok, we've all got fun stuff to do. And no one to bitch at about it for two weeks."

Talking about the last one hundred years inevitably means talking about how Karma is possibly a real thing- something real in the world.

In 2032, Earth hit a kind of weird milestone in the form of its very first Trillionaire. If you aren't a big number person, imagine a Trillion dollars as if there were ten billion people on a planet and every one of them, men, women, and children, pulled out their wallet and gave you 100 dollars.

So, it's a lot.

To be accurate, this trillionaire, in his first year as a member of the "T' club, had 1.2 Trillion dollars.

So now imagine all those people pulling out an extra twenty.

This milestone coincided with a record number of people, all across the planet, who were experiencing severe poverty. Over two billion people were going to sleep hungry, a large number of them children.

People with empathy were pretty upset. And that was a surprisingly large number of them. But there were still a lot of people who didn't care. People who would say things like, "Maybe don't have children if you can't afford them."

That probably sounds like a dickish thing to say. And it is, but it may be even more unaware than it is unkind. Sociologists had been saying for a long time that human beings had two reproductive strategies, both instinctive and situational.

In the first, when resources are high, humans have one or two children and they take very good care of them. You see this across developing countries where the top 50% of the population or so in terms of income will have few children and expend considerable resources keeping them safe.

In the second, when resources are low or absent, humans will have many children and then hope that some survive. It turns out that family planning is a process that requires resources.

Family planning costs money.

So Malthusian predictions about the population started to come true. If resources were allocated in a responsible way, the earth could have handled ten billion people. But the way it was, ten billion people was a disaster. As the population skyrocketed, so did disease, stress but on utilities, water spoilage, ecological damage. And this impacted even the very wealthy.

By the time governments acted on it, there were Five trillionaires worldwide. Their wealth was over eight trillion dollars. And, again, as a reference, there is about seven point five trillion dollars worth of gold in the entire world. And five people had more cash than that.

By 2060, nations of the world had finally identified the super-wealthy as a threat, hoarding money, resources, and land that we desperately needed for the survival of large swatches of people. They applied a cap to wealth. And the twenty-five hundred people above that cap ended up stripped of trillions of dollars. Don't worry, though. They were still obscenely wealthy. Just not encumbered with "Fuck you, planet" money.

Money that would eventually be used to find a solution.

Money was used to feed and clothe, house and educate people who needed it. And, sure enough, the population started to level out. But what to do with the massive number of people on the planet already?

It was decided that generation ships would be sent to nearby planets, filled with people who wanted to try a new planet, a different one. They would be put into suspended animation and sleep their way to a new world.

This helped get people off the planet quickly. But what was going to happen when they arrived?

Would they just show up to a raw world?

The Generation ships would take decades to get there. Work began on smaller ships. These very small ships would travel far faster, bringing newer technology, including methods to terraform and build. These smaller ships left later and made the trip much faster, traveling many times the speed of light to the destination where they could use more modern technology to make the colonists' lives easier.

The ships were tiny, though. And what it took to get them off earth couldn't be replicated on the other side. So it was a one way trip for everyone. This meant that all of us who were assigned to these ships had to be ready to make a new life. We had to have skills that would add to life in the new colony. We had to be people who could live for a year or so in tiny spaces. And we had to be people committed to the cause- getting people to a new world. That means you need a little bit of protector in you.

Just a little bit.

If that sounds like me, I'm ok with that. My life has been spent in space. And the rest of it, after we land, is going to be spent making Centauri B livable, prosperous, and kind.

That's a goal I can get behind.

"Come," I addressed the buzz at my door.

Marin and Lyra walked in.

Lyra looked around, "Huh. I thought this would be bigger."

"My pod is the same size as all of them."

"That's why you'd make a terrible Pirate."

"I like to think there are a lot of reasons. What do you got?"

Marin held up a glass tube. In it was what looked like half a teaspoon of goo. "Well, not much, but it's worth a discussion."

"So discuss with me. What is it?"

"It's undifferentiated tissue."

"Stem cells" I knew what those were.

"Basically. Like cells you might find in an umbilical cord."

"Ok, so these are human cells?"

"They are."

"How did they get there? Why aren't they in someone's body?"

Marin and Lyra exchanged a glance.

"We don't know."

"So, what's the discussion about?"

"Well, we do need to find out how they got there and why. But we know the who."

"What do you mean? The cells. Whose are they?"

Lyra handed me the tube. "Yours, captain."

"They're yours."

-15 Days

"Can someone tell me why we haven't tossed this fucking thing out the side port." Roja was standing around the galley table in the den along with the rest of us, looking for a quick solution to something I didn't understand yet. And Kalista agreed.

"I'm absolutely wondering the same thing. At this point, I don't really care where this all came from."

"Trust me, that's not my issue, honestly." Although I really was interested in figuring out what the hell was happening.

Dae was concerned but also looked willing to find solutions, "So this thing doubled in mass overnight?"

Lyra had a point to make though, "Look, this is freaking me out, too. I don't know where this came from. These are like HeLa cells, in a way. They aren't dying. They're growing. But they're also undifferentiated. This is like a supply of stem cells coded to the captain. I mean, I could technically grow you a new spine with this."

Marin jumped in, "If you needed it."

"Well, I don't. I think. I think my spine is working just fine."

Dae got closer to the tube. "You could clone her from this?"

Lyra continued, "I absolutely could. Anyone could. And the cells have a blisteringly fast replication rate."

"So, we have to get rid of it. Or it takes over the ship"

"Not necessarily, Marin countered.It's healthy cells. Not cancer. It will stop growing when it needs to stop."

"You're acting like it has a mind and everything?"

Marin was fascinated by this. It was obvious. And I suspected I knew why. About fifty years ago, undifferentiated cells turned out to be the solution to creating a real, stable, and sustainable gender affirmation mode. Marin, as a trans man, owed a lot of his current welfare to undifferentiated cells like this. He recognized their value.

"Not a mind, no. But healthy cells actually stop growing when they reach the limits of their plan or enclosing area. These are undifferentiated so they have no specific plan.But they do have a bounding area. Healthy cells play by a kind of "covenant" with other cells- they agree to do their jobs. Cancerous cells ignore all that. They just keep growing."

Roja was impressed, "The most words you've said the entire time you've been here." He reached out to high five him. Marin wearily gave in and did it.

"So they should stop growing in the tube eventually?"

"Yes. And, I mean, these are you. These could be used alongside gene therapy to cure anything that really afflicted you. We could throw them away, but to you, to your body, this is a priceless treasure."

"That could engulf the ship, taking iit over and eventually destroy it."

Lyra sighed and thought, "I doubt that, Captain."

"What do you think?" I looked over at Marin. I wanted my biologist's opinion, too.

"I think I'd like to study it more. I can't imagine that this is something we need to worry about. And maybe there is something in there we can use."

Kalista looked at Roja who was quiet for once,

"I can't tell you you have to get rid of it. I mean, This is a scientific finding that a lot of people back on earth would go nuts for. But, still. I think you should eject it."

"Hell, yeah." Roja was being overly protective of the ship, I suspected. But were Lyra and Marin beijing overly incautious because it was a find? I didn't know.

"Ok, you two, take Kalista and study it. You have 24 hours and then if you can't tell me how it got here it goes out the port. Is that cool?"

"Yes, sir."

"I'll see you guys at dinner."

Dae was subdued as she walked with me back to my quarters. I could tell she had mixed feelings.

"Let me ask you a question."

We had just stepped into my quarters, "Shoot."

"If you could change one thing about me, what would it be?"

"This is the worst Vogue quiz ever."

"I'm serious. Using stem cells like that, they can clone someone and leave them as is, or remove a certain property in a clone. Let's say you're making clones of me. What do you change before I notice? Before I open my eyes."

"I can't imagine there is any good answer to this. But wait, in this scenario, I'm making multiple versions? Please, go on?"

"Like a harem of me." she laughed.

"Suddenly I'm into this line of questioning."

"But for real. I'm trying to trip you up or anything. But we've been dating for a while, what do you change?"

"Stop it."

"No, seriously, I want to know."

"I would make you take a hint and shut up when we're answering horrible hypothetical questions. I would give you an off switch. But, no, you're perfect the way you are. I wouldn't say no to two of you, though, let's keep that option open. That sounds like Saturday night to me."

I kissed her. The goal was to calm any insecurity that was causing her to ask questions like this. But I recognized that it could come off as manipulative.

"I've changed since I've been with you." she wasn't wrong, but I was curious if she saw what I did.

"Oh, yeah, how?"

"Do you see it?"

"I know what I think. What do you think?"

"I think you should pay attention closely. I don't want to go back."

Her hair was black and dense and longer even than I remembered. I felt something when she turned around. Maybe a kind of desperation. Something unusual. Like I wanted her to face me, but I didn't know how to make that work.

"I wouldn't mind being taller. I wouldn't mind being a little bigger in general."

"Oh, yeah." I thought she was just being sexy and playful.

"I wouldn't mind staying." She put her hands on my breasts.

"I was hoping you would stay." I pulled off her shirt.

She looked at me as if I'd missed a big part of that conversation and I wasn't sure I hadn't.

"The truth is that we WEREN'T a research vessel. We were under no obligation to explore or run experiments or anything. We were absolutely within our rights to just ignore anomalies and gloss over everything that wasn't part of our core mission- to get planetside and prepare it for the generation ship.

But the industry of space, to which we all belonged, was rooted deeply in the idea of research, exploration. The goal of constantly researching the unknown was sort of built into the idea with such strength that it was hard for any of us to turn our backs on a mystery.

Even when it was absurd and impossible.

We had spent a good part of the afternoon in bed, just cuddling, reading, doing some research. Dae stood up and made a purposeful walk to the bathroom and back in her underwear. She really was adorable.

She returned and asked.

"I thought our pods were all the same size."

I thought for a second. Had Lyra commented on that yesterday? "They are."

"No. Yours is a tiny bit bigger.

"It may just seem that way. I'm constantly moving the furniture around here to see if I can get more space. I think I landed on this layout because it feels larger. "

"I never noticed until today. But it's bigger"

I called up the specs on my tablet and showed her. It testified to the fact that all pods were the same size. Each pod was 4 meters by 5 meters.

Pretty much exactly. Each pod was based on a kind of symmetry so it wouldn't make sense if they were different sizes.

Dae looked over my shoulder. "It says it, but... I'm not sure I buy it. I think this room is bigger.

"I don't know what to tell you." I thought for a second. I think this was just the diversion we both needed. I grabbed her hand.

"Where are we going?"

"C'mon."

I met Dae while we were all training on the smaller ships. She was on the build team for the new line of hyperfast ships so she got to run people through their paces.

The Large Generation ships used standard drives and would take, in some cases, decades, to reach their destinations. But these smaller ships were built around Alcubierre drives.

The drive itself is named for the person who first pioneered this method, way back in the 20th century,.

in 1994, a there was a Mexican physicist named F Miguel Alcubierre who sort of proposed a new method by which people could travel. He wanted to stretch the fabric of space-time in a way which would theoretically allow for faster than light travel.

The idea was to create an artifact that contracted space in front of them and expanded it behind, creating a sort of do it yourself warp bubble that could enclose and carry the ships in a multiple of lightspeed. And while the passengers wouldn't necessarily experience time dilation, they would be cut off from anything outside their bubble for weeks at a time during transit.

Any object inside this wave would sort of ride this bubble like a surfer, enclosed by the curve of the contraction.

This became known as the "Alcubierre Metric" in General Relativity, this metric permits a warp bubble to sort of appear in an unmanipulated, flat region of spacetime and move away, at speeds faster than the speed of light like a carbonation bubble on the top of a glass of soda. The inside of the bubble is the inertial reference frame for any object inhabiting it, because it's a closed system. So no heavy Gravity like effects.

The ship itself is not moving within the bubble, which is. It is being carried along as the "world" it occupies itself moves, so conventional relativistic effects such as time dilation don't apply. So, no violation of the laws of general relativity.

NASA sent Nanocrafts using this method for years, tiny tiny unmanned ships. They helped pave the way for larger and larger successful flights. Eventually, about fifty years ago, the first manned ship was sent, with an astronaut named Mira Ardoni. The ship was lost and she, as far as anyone knew, was splattered across the inside of the Hypersurface of the Bubble and atomized on reentry.

As a testament to the perseverance of humanity, five more people died before the process was perfected. Building the Alcubierre bubble required a lot of energy and it wasn't terribly stable. So, now, fifty some years later the ships that can manage it aren't much bigger. They just work a bit better.

I tell you this because you need to understand that the entire time Dae was explaining it to me, she had her hand on my lower back and was moving her fingers back and forth in a way that prevented me from taking in any new information at all.

She had introduced herself when I arrived. Her name was Daewon Park, although her friends called her Dae. She was some combination that included Korean, although, at this point in history everyone on earth knew more about their genetics from at-home kits than from their faces.

It was virtually impossible to tell where anyone's ancestors had come from hundreds of years ago. I know I was part Jamaican and part Japanese, but, in all honesty, my last name "Kimura" was more Japanese than any part of me you could photograph or draw. I enjoyed a good anima movie and a sushi dinner. But so did everyone else, really.

She was a few inches smaller than me and had the most remarkable smile. When she did, her whole face opened up and only the dark, glossy, pretty parts of her eyes showed. She was seemingly quiet with other people but almost effulgent with me. She later told me that I made her want to talk because I so obviously loved listening to her. And that observation demonstrated that she was paying attention with that scientist's eye.

She loved to fly and one of our first dates was on the JPL / NASA lot, flying one of the planes that she had access to. So when I had a short mission inside the solar system I chose her to pilot. We used an older ship and did a loop around Titan. The dense gravity wells on the ship created just enough time dilation that the two of us were now younger by a few days than the other things around us our age when we left. It's a weird thing to bond over but it works. We went out dancing and felt young.

Younger than anything else in the world.

We started spending all our time together. We both loved to travel which was another thing to bond over.

I had met Kalista in college and we became instant rivals and friends. We pushed each other to excel. She was generalist, a scientist who picked up information easily about nearly everything and never put it back down again. And while Dae was densely into Physics, I was more of a student of people. I loved working with people, mentoring people, getting the best out of people. We fell really naturally into our roles. And that may be one reason why the three of us because such close friends.

It was easy for Dae and myself to drag Kalista with on our trips. She added a lot of whimsy and silliness and never tried to get in between us or soften the sharp edges of our relationship. Kalista was enough of a loner that she loved exploring places without us.

The three of us spent a full week in Strasbourg, spending time in Petite France, the Tanneurs district, and the Vauban Dam, Dae and I wandered around Neustadt while Kalista made new friends in the Grande Île and we all met up again at the Notre-Dame Cathedral, under its great massive stone and glass walls and got famously drunk.

We fought the overwhelming crowds of people that had grown up around us as we visited the world, I think, each of us knowing that we would one day leave it. And as we watched the giant generation ships take off, each with over ten thousand souls asleep for decades, we had an idea of how we might do it.

To be there for those people when they arrived. To make their new lives into something good.

I dragged Dae to her pod. I realized now that I'd only stepped foot in it a few times since we left. She spent nearly every night in my pod with me. I silently decided to address that. I can't make her feel like she's always coming to me, always trying to be in my world.

I have to do better than that.

I squeezed her hand and stepped in.

The pod was fairly sparse. I had expected to see more of her in it, more expressions of the Ddae that I knew. But there were books, plain, NASA standard issued sheets, not too much that might distinguish it from other pods.

Except I knew Dae better than that. Right away I could see that her bed held about twice as many pillows as the Pods came with. This was how she had been since I met her. At her own place I would often have to navigate all the pillows that she would wrap around herself every night to sleep, like a tiny fort that welcomed her and protected her.

The color scheme was dark. Blacks and dark blues.

This was no doubt meant to provide a comfortable space when she was dealing with one of her infrequent migraines, debilitating headaches that made it hard for her to function.

But she did.

I found, after this last three years, that often the only way I could tell if she was having one was the ever so slight squint in her eyes as she went about her day, restricting light, calming her brain, making it possible for her to see at all.

The smell of lemon was commonplace, too. Dae loved scents and citrus ones were what she gravitated toward always. An infuser on the shelf sat next to Brazilian orange oil, grapefruit oil, lemon and a lime basil that sounded interesting. I made a point to focus more on scents in my pod. At least I could make her feel more at home.

"So what do you think?"

"I don't know. It looks about the same size."

"Is that really what you think?"

I stepped back and really looked. In all honesty, it's not what I thought. My knee jerk instinct, my first assessment, was that it felt smaller.

It felt a little smaller.

"Is this a ridiculous thing to focus on?" she wrapped her arms around me.

"Well, it's certainly not something we can do much about. But maybe it's the layout. Do you think that the way it's laid out is making us feel like it's smaller?"

"It could be." there were really only a few items in the room. But that seemed like the only answer.

"C'mon," I took her hand and we moved the bed against the far wall. That wouldn't make a huge difference. So we moved the desk aside and slid it up against the long wall, butting the head up against the shorter wall.

We moved the desk next to it and the armoire/entertainment center in front of the bed, up against the wall.

This was the exact layout of my pod. There are really only three items in these things so it had to be the same.

Dae walked to the area at the foot of the bed.

Ok, in yours, this space is bigger. This whole area here is definitely about ten centimeters bigger.

"That's not possible." I flopped on the bed and looked around. The goal here was to put this whole thing to rest but it didn't do that at all. She was right, I could tell.

This was smaller.

-14 Days

Roja was working on the Den table. He'd been trying to make it into a standing/sitting table. He had a tendency to leave a little chaos in his wake during these big projects, but they calmed him. If he couldn't build things or fix things he would go silently insane and I suspect he might take the rest of us with him. So we all just nodded when he suggested these remodeling projects and tried to live in the future, when it was done and we were reaping the benefits.

"So you guys tossed it?"

"Yep," Marin got some juice out of the cold storage unit and sat down out of the way.

I looked around, "So where is Lyra?"

"She's not feeling great today so she may stay in her pod for a bit."

"Is that anything I should be worried about?" I looked down at my bowl. I knew it was oatmeal but for a moment it didn't look like it. A trick of the light.

"No, I'll let you know if it gets worse."

Kalista wandered in, still half asleep. "If you are the stand-in doctor, I need drugs."

Marin chuckled, "Are you drug-seeking?"

"Abso-fucking-lutely."

I stepped over to where Roja was working and leaned in. "Hey, Acosta"

He looked up. "Uh oh. Using my last name. I'm in trouble."

"No, no, not at all. I wanted to ask you a really stupid question."

"I'm here for stupid, my captain."

"Ok. Is it at all possible that one of the pods is bigger than another one?"

"Bigger? No. The ship is symmetrical across a lateral axis. There should be no way one could be bigger than another one."

"Ok, that's what I thought. It's stupid."

"Do you think that one is bigger?"

"I stayed in Dae's pod last night and she is absolutely convinced that mine is bigger."

"Well, that's not possible." He sat up and looked at me. "I mean, you move stuff around in yours all the time. Are you sure it doesn't just LOOK bigger?"

"Yeah, I thought of that."

"Well. let's go measure it."

The hardest part of being the captain is knowing how to act like you don't feel stupid when you really, really do. Roja was explaining, on the way, how completely standardized all these bubble drive ships had become.

"They can strip them down considerably, because there really should be no G-force inertial effects.

And we're out of phase with all the outside radiation so only the reactor in the ship, that's in the bubble, can potentially cause any radiation damage. Any small object is diverted by the bubble, and larger ones glance off. And the ships carry the same skillsets for helping to terraform and model the planets for the colonists, Command, General Science, Medical, Life Science, and Technology."

He had been counting off on his fingers and it made him almost drop his tool bag.

"Ok, so NASA LOOOOVES standardized things. Give them something that has been proven to work and keep people alive and does the job and they will reuse the shit out of it. Don't get me wrong, they love inventing shit. But only when they need to."

We were at my pod and I realized that outside of Dae, nobody else had really been in it for a while. Had I been keeping everyone at arm's length for weeks? It's possible. These people were supposed to be my friends, too.

"How long have we known each other?"

Roja snorted. "Oh, jesus. You and Kal and I did our first post together probably twelve years ago. We did that Lunar thing."

"Right. The Blue area experiment. That was fun."

"You started out as XO but you were captain by the end of it."

"Who knew Leland would get so sick in real low G?"

"I did. That motherfucker was throwing up during training"

He looked around.

"Well, at first glance, it does seem roomy in here."

"Dae says that this area here at the foot of the bed is too wide."

"It should be a meter. These giant fucking beds are three meters long and the multi-cab is half a meter deep. "

One of the things that the various space organizations had discovered in the last fifty years was that a large and comfortable bed solved many problems. For some reason, people were willing to accommodate some discomfort in other areas for a large comfy bed. So they had developed these special outsized beds with headrests and automated lighting and movement. During downtime, many people were able to stay in bed and read. The combination of turning one full wall into a monitor that could express an outdoor scene and a bed you just wanted to stay in could apparently make nearly any imposition worth it.

"So this area here should be a meter and a half."

"Yes, it should be one hundred and fifty centimeters."

"And it is?"

"One hundred and fifty seven point five centimeters."

"Shit."

That's when we heard the alarm.

Roja and I quickly moved to the den. Everyone was there but Lyra.

"Can someone turn that off?" I had never heard this particular alarm before but I knew that whatever it was warning us about could be more easily addressed without it.

"What is it?" Roja started rustling through the files on the screen above the galley table to figure it out.

Kalista had already done the work, "It's the alarm for initiating extraction."

"And what the hell is that?"

Roja had found the same information, apparently. He turned it off. "It's part of a new series of protocols. It looks like it's an accident. It seems like it went off randomly."

I sighed, "ok, I officially hate this. Is Lyra still out?"

Marin pointed to a screen to one side of the room that showed the slight redhead looking down, "I'm sorry, Captain. I'm feeling a little fluish and I don't want to infect anyone. I'm here and available, though."

"Do you know what this alarm is?"

"It says it's a medical protocol but I'm not familiar. I'm researching now."

"Good. get some rest and feel better. But simultaneously find out what that alarm is and what 'extraction' it's talking about"

"Ayes, Captain." and the screen went black.

"Today we're going to do a full sweep of this shop for anything out of the ordinary. Three anomalous things have happened in as many days…"

"What's the third?" Kalista looked at me.

Roja held up his measuring tape. "Her pod is officially seven and a half centimeters bigger than the others."

Dae had been leaning quietly up against the wall. "Wait, I was right?"

"Oh, shut up, you're always right, bitch." Kalista slapped her arm.

"Yeah, Dae, I need that scientist's eye. Something fucked up is going on and I want to find out what. Not tomorrow. Not next week. Today."

I looked around the room. Marin spoke up, "on it, captain."

"You don't like sleeping in my pod, do you?"

I shined the light at Dae and took the bait. "Why do you say that, little girl?"

She was crouched down next to me in the maintenance tubes. There wasn't much room in here for a conversation.

"You were tossing and turning. Did you have the dream?"

I admit that I had been having the dream about the girl in the pool more than usual. I suspect it was the claustrophobia of the ship that was to blame. The idea of dying, trapped, no air, in full view of all those people, that may have resonated a lot with someone like me who was raised with the idea of going into space.

"Maybe. But I'm having other bad dreams."

"You didn't tell me that."

"It's not a big deal. They are mostly things that didn't happen."

I turned to her and sat. Sitting cross legged, both of us could talk fairly comfortably in the tube.

"Dae, did we ever see a horror movie together about a brain surgery?"

"Um. Is there one in Dr. Aligro's Cage?"

"No, I remember that. He was cutting off people's body parts. That was a fucked up movie, why did we see that?"

"Oh, you liked it. How about 'Hunt'"

"Oh, yeah, they took that guy's brain out entirely."

"It looked smooth."

"Did you actually lose respect for the guy because his brain didn't look striated enough."

"I think i did."

"Hm. Maybe that was it."

"What was your dream?"

Ever since I was a kid I had been cursed with a pretty accurate recall of dreams, no matter how stupid or terrifying. This one was a little from both columns.

"That sounds bad."

"It was ok. But it didn't help me sleep, even though I was in the actual pillow factory."

"Pillows are love, Zedi."

"I know. I know, sweety."

"Tell me."

I took a deep breath. I certainly never wanted to put any imagery into people's heads that didn't grow there organically. And this was stupid.

"Ok, the whole thing is like a movie, but from my point of view. I feel, in the dream, like I'm trapped in my head. I look down at my hands and I'm holding a little black box. I was holding it tightly because there are creases in my hand, like red marks from holding on to it so tightly.

I step into a waiting room. It's all white. Everything is white. It's a waiting area for a doctor, I think. The receptionist doesn't look me in the eye. I sit down and wait. There is only one other person in there. A woman wearing a pink knit hat. I look up at the back of her head and it looks like there are a few drops of blood dripping from under the hat.

I get up and run to the bathroom. I run the water. Looking up in the mirror, it looks like I've been crying. So I wipe my face off."

"This is all still the same dream?"

"Yes. I know, it's dumb, but wait. I go back and the nurse calls me in. It's a perfectly white operating room and I step up on the table. There are straps on the side and the nurse comes in and straps me in. I'm still fully dressed and all and it just feels not right. I look around for the doctor and I see a kind of mirror up above the operating room table. It's just a little off, making it impossible for me to see my face in it.

Then the doctor comes in. He doesn't say anything. He's quick and he pulls the straps tighter, until I can't move at all. I try to be calm and then I feel this pressure on my head. It smells like burning meat and I twist a little. The nurse forces me to stay still and accidentally bumps the overhead mirror. And I can see it."

"You see what?"

"This is the fucked up part. It's the doctor pulling off the top of my head and putting the black box inside. There's no room for it but he presses down."

"That's horrible."

"I see it for a split second and then it's over."

"You have this dream a lot?"

"Not really, just a few times here or there."

"We can stay in your pod from now on."

"What if I got more pillows?"

"That's always a plus. You know that."

"I don't want you to think I'm not comfortable in your world. I don't want to be the one in this relationship that requires that you come to me."

"You know, honestly, it's not a big deal. Do you want me around?"

"Every minute. It's scary how much I want you around."

"Then that's all I need."

Just then, my com buzzed. Roja's voice rang out. "Captain, You want to be notified about anomalies?"

"I do, Ro, what is it?"

"Come and meet us in the area between the stem and the transom way."

I thought about the layout of the ship. "There is no area between the stem and the transom way."

"Well, there is now. Follow my ping."

I looked at Dae, "what the fuck."

We followed Acosta's com link back to an area on the other side of the ship. He was holding a tablet out for me.

"What am I looking at?"

He pointed. "This is an area about the size of a closet. I swear to god it wasn't there a few days ago. There's no entry or exit. It's just a tiny closed off room.

Kalista looked as confused as I felt. "We measured around it and looked at all the ship plans. It's definitely there, but it wasn't before."

"What are the chances that the software was updated somewho to register this space and it just didn't list it before? Or we're in a more precise mode or something."

Roja looked though the tablet, "I guess, but it's listed as secure storage. Why would that have been hidden before?"

"What's it storing, "asked Dae. This was a pretty good question.

Kalista ran down the list, "It's not food, it's not gear, it's not personal effects. All those things have storage facilities that we know about."

"Why hide a storage room?"

"Even better," Roja looked up, "Why make a storage area with no access."

"So, wait, there is no access to this room?

Dae was looking through the tablet, trying to make sense of it. Rojass pointed.

"Not from inside."

"I just want to go on record saying that I hate this."

"Hate it, too, captain, but this is necessary."

"Your presence on this ship is far more necessary than knowing what's in that little space."

Kalista interjected, "Unless it's a security risk that could jeopardize the mission.

"And what are the chances of that?" I was about a minute away from putting my foot down on this.

"I don't know. I just don't."

"Dae, what do you think about an EVA while we're in transit?"

She looked at me. "It should be totally safe. We're not really moving. It's the Alcubierre bubble that's moving. We're in a closed system. The bubble extends about ten meters out from the ship in every direction. So, as long as he stays tethered and doesn't wander outside the bubble, he's fine. He won't even feel any motion. It will be like a stationary satellite based maneuver. "

"Ten meters is a lot. My tether will only be a few meters long. I basically can't reach the edge of the bubble.

I wasn't satisfied. "And what happens if a part of his body gets caught outside the bubble?"

Dae looked pained, "Well, inside the bubble we are totally stationary with respect to what's around us. There is even a bit of an atmosphere that we captured on takeoff. Not breathable, but not a pressure problem, either."

"And outside?"

"Outside the right at the surface, the outside is effectively moving at a speed that is maybe one hundred times the speed of light. So anything that passed through the membrane would be sheared off completely and suffer massive time dilation at the same time. Also, space."

"See why I'm not excited?"

"Captain, Zed, I can do this easily. And I'll be right back. I'll have a camera the whole time and I'll be tethered the whole time. It'll take me longer to put the suit on than the whole trip will take."

"I'm inclined to want to nix this. Or go myself."

"I think that would be a bad idea, Captain. Something very odd is going on here, and information is all we really have." Kalista sounded earnest.

I looked over at Dae, "I think she's right, Captain."

I sighed," Ok, get Marin down there, too, waiting. I want SOMEBODY with medical training when you get back, even if Lyra is not available. "

Kalista had helped Roja get into the suit. The modern suits were not overly bulky, but they did take two people to completely close. Marin sat nearby with a medkit.

"Can you see the camera, Cap?"

"Yep. Looking good."

Dae and I were in the den, watching on the big monitor.

We could see Roja's face in the secondary monitor while the main one just showed what he was looking at.

"Looking a little red."

"I'm excited. Is this the most distant EVA in the history of man?"

"Now I see why we're doing this."

"I'm just saying, it's pretty impressive."

I shook my head, "Yeah, well, stay tethered."

De and I watched as he opened the airlock and stepped out, locking the tetherline to one of the thin but strong rods that encircled the ship. These were specifically made to take a tether and there was one that ran right near the area he was going to investigate.

"Looking good, Ro." I realized that I hadn't been breathing until he clicked the lock on the tetherline. It was brutal just to be sitting here watching it. This was my ship. I understood that this was his area of expertise.

"So far, so good." he moved slowly and cautiously across the hull until he was near the door that led into the mysterious storage space.

He moved along a few feet over and opened the outer lock on the space.

"I have two options here, Captain. I can untether and - "

"Absolutely not."

"Hear me out. The rim of this is a little sharp. If I keep the tether on, I run the risk of damaging it on the port rim. Or I can remove and retract it and reattach it inside the space."

"Or you could come back right now."

"This is easy, Captain, I don't want to die, trust me. There is no danger here. Just don't make any sharp turns."

"Ha." I turned the intercom off and spoke to Dae, "tell me this is a good idea."

"It's actually fine. He's only untethered for a few seconds and then he's attached again. Same thing with the way out. The ship really can't jar or bump."

"Fuck." I switched the intercom back on, "Ok, if you are comfortable, reattach as fast as you can inside the space.

"Yep. Got it." He detached and quickly reattached the tether under the air lock hinge."

"Damn."

"What damn."

the feed went black.

"Goddamnit. Kal, what's going on over there?"

"Hold on. It's ok. He's ok.

The feed kicked back in.

"Sorry. This tether snapped. I'm connected to the one below it. I'm ok."

"Fuck. I hate this."

"It's ok. "

We waited for a moment.

"Done. closing the airlock. "

We hadn't read any atmosphere in the storage space so He kept the suit on even as he closed the airlock. At first it was too dark to register anything in the space

"I'm turning up my suitlights." As Rojas moved his head around, we could see what he was seeing.

The room seemed empty. It was about 1 meter square and nearly twenty feet high, the height of all internal space in the ship. That made it look huge. "I don't see anything"

"Ro, look to your left."

We could see it now, a series of small, 5 x 5 centimeter blocks, slightly recessed in the wall. "Do you see that?"

"Yep. closing in." From this distance we could see the impressions around them. They were some kind of drawer.

"Storage units?" He speculated.

"Tiny ones. Can you see what they say?"

Yes. Do you see?"

We could read them now. There were five of them. Kimura, Collins, Ayala, Acosta, Tambor."

Those were our last names. The last names of the people on the ship.

Dae read them.

"Where's Park?"

I looked at the footage to see if we missed it.

There's one for everyone on the ship." She paused. She looked heartbroken.

"Except me."

-13 Days

I woke up to Dae sitting on the bed, staring at the doll on my desk. "I can't believe you still have this."

I wrapped my arms around her waist and slid over to her, "Of course I do. That was the first thing you ever gave me. From the market in Taiwan."

"It's looking a little beat up."

"Haven't you read the Velveteen Rabbit? You know how these things work." I held on to her and she kissed my head. I could tell she had something on her mind and I was afraid I knew what it was.

"I have this weird feeling I don't belong here."

"Of course you do. Jesus, no one knows more about this ship than you do. You and Ro could practically build one together in your sleep."

"We could. Definitely, but, it's just been gnawing at me."

"Since yesterday?"

"Honestly, since before that. Before. But, yesterday, that was fucked up."

"You want to know why your name wasn't in that room?"

"Wouldn't you?"

"Except that room means nothing. I swear to god it wasn't even on the specs until yesterday."

"That's not possible."

"Well, how possible is it that you don't belong here?"

"I don't know. I just don't"

"You belong right here. With me. I think you know that. But right now, it's 6 am, I think we both belong in bed."

"Ha. are you trying to coerce me into bed?"

"I'm the captain. I can just order you if I need to."

"Oh, yeah? Like with a stern voice?"

"I'm going to need you to behave."

She stared at me for a moment. There was something I felt like she wanted to say but it was going to take time. It didn't bother me much.

We had time.

"Thank you. I appreciate you. I know you're trying to make me feel better."

"There's no reason for you to be upset. I know this feeling is just hanging on, but that's all it is. A feeling."

I grabbed her hands and squeezed tight. "This is where you belong. And people need you."

She slid back into bed and we slept for another hour or two, with her head nuzzled into my neck.

I caught her spinning around in the area between the bed and the multi when I woke up.

"So much room."

"It is almost eight centimeters bigger than yours, so..."

"You're going to think I'm crazy."

"I already do," I hugged her and gave her a big kiss on the nose.

"It looks bigger today."

"Oh, come on."

"It does. Tell me what you think."

I looked down. She wasn't totally wrong.

The center of the ship was called the Den. Research into space travel had shown that separating the lounge areas and the functional areas of the ship made the people running the ship nervous. They didn't want to spend time in the lounge where they wouldn't be able to respond to a problem. But being in the functional, control areas of the ship constantly was draining.

The Den was the solution. Think of it as a duplex apartment. The front area was the control space for the ship. This was mostly necessary during takeoff and landing. It had monitors and equipment needed to manage the mechanisms all over the ship. Right behind it, if you stepped up, was the galley. This included a large central table and food storage areas, both hot and stable, with cooking equipment.

Behind that, if you stepped down again, was the lounge with a couch and a central wall monitor. Showers and bathrooms branched off of that. This entire structure sat central along the midline of the ship, with pods on either side. It was not large. For decades, thought these Bubble ships had been tiny, mostly one person ships. The specs for this, in comparison, were excessive.

Massive.

"So what do you guys think those were?" Ro was piling food on top of more food in the Den.

I walked in with Dae right behind, "I thought we made our guesses last night"

Marin looked up. "I think he has new, fun ideas."

"That's right, I do."

"Well, all right. Breakfast is the most important meal of the day. Let's hear them."

Roja seemed a little too excited. "It's a spandrel."

"I can honestly say that's the first time I've ever heard that word. I think you're making it up."

Kalista shot back, "Because that's a dumb idea."

Marin cocked his head. I looked over at him. "What? You agree?"

"I think it's an option."

Rojas continued. "They use the word in biology to mean something similar. In architecture, a spandrel is an accidental shape that's made in construction when you create necessary structures. Like the triangles in the corner when you build an arch in a square area. I think that this space was just an accidental feature of the build of the ship."

"And why does it have all of your names in it but mine?"

"I think they inscribed it with the names of the non-engineers who were going to be on the ship. As a kind of good luck. You're an engineer. So they left you out."

"Does that sound reasonable to you?"

"Do you have any better ideas?"

I sighed. "No, I do not. But…"

Kalista stared at me. "You do, don't you?"

"No. Really. I don't." I sighed. "Look, I'm going to ask a question that is going to seem insane. And it's going to make me sound like I don't know anything about how science works. So I need you guys to not completely disrespect me."

I looked around. "Wait, where is Lyra?"

Marin shook his head. "Still sick?"

"Yeah, I don't like that." I spoke louder, "Lyra's room."

There was a buzz. No answer.

"Is she sleeping?"

"Maybe. Visual on pod three."

The monitor remained black. A blinking sign in the center said "Privacy enabled."

"I like that even less." I started off to Lyra's pod. I realized I'd never been in her pod before. I tried to think back to when we were prepping the ship and I drew a blank.

Had I never gone into her pod?

Ro followed me, with the rest not far behind. I knocked on Lyra's door.

No answer.

"Lyra, are you ok? Marin, when was the last time you checked on her?"

"I talked to her on monitor last night. She said she was feeling better."

"Well, this isn't better. Lyra!"

I looked at Rojas, "Can you open this door?"

"Not if she's on privacy."

"Ok, but can you open the door?"

"Yes."

"Do it."

He took out a tiny tool and pulled it open, pressing one part of it to the door seam. A screen lit up in the tool and he tapped it.

The door swung open.

It was dark. At first glance it looked like any other pod.

Until you walked in.

The pods were meant to be about four meters by five. This one was square. And it seemed to measure about six meters both ways.

It was some 16 square meters bigger than mine.

And it was about five degrees warmer.

There was a shape hiddled in the corner. I reached for the light but it didn't turn on.

I pulled out my light and flipped it on. Lyra's voice rung out, "don't"

Suddenly I felt something hit me in the ribs. I started to fall, grabbing at whatever did it. I grabbed an arm. It was warm and covered in thick sweat. The arm tried to pull away.

I yanked hard and the figure fell backward. I got down on one knee and tried to hold it down.

"Lyra. Stop. What are you doing?"

Dae flipped her light on and I saw the petite redhead under me, breathing heavily.

"She's warm. I think she has a fever."

"I'm sorry, captain. I'm sorry."

"Marin, are you able to grab her?"

"Got it."

Kalista's voice rang out. "Holy shit."

I got up and turned. "What the fuck."

Kal's light was illuminating her face. "Zed."

I followed her, "What's going on?"

Kal looked spooked. "I don't want to be crazy here, but that's not a clump of cells anymore."

She flashed her light on Lyra's Desk, on which was a large tube containing the cells she was supposed to have thrown out.

"That's a fucking baby."

"What the fuck were you thinking?"

"I don't know. I just. It started growing and I couldn't just throw it out." Lyra was shivering, holding a blanket around herself.

"So you lied to my face and kept something potentially dangerous from me."

"I'm sorry."

She seemed so fragile. Something was going on with her. It wasn't just the fever. I made a note to go through her file tonight. What made her so attached to this, especially after it started to look like an actual fetus."

"Why the dark?"

"It grows in the dark. It seemed to need it. "

The cylinder containing the fetus was sitting in the middle of the Galley table now. We were all a bit jumpy. Especially Kal, "Well, that's not creepy at all."

"Why would it grow better in the dark?"

I looked at Marin and he shrugged.

Lyra offered up, "I don't really know."

Dae asked the question that was on my mind, "so, is this a clone?"

Marin responded, "Cloning is pretty commonplace now and this," he waved his hand, "is not how we do it."

Roja was very concerned about the other thing we'd seen, "And why is your Pod nearly twice as large as the others?"

Kal looked at him and he put his hand up, "Yes, not twice, I know math, but much much bigger."

"I don't know." Lyra fumbled, "I haven't seen the others."

"Was it always that big?"

"I don't know. I haven't thought about it. No, But that's crazy."

"It is crazy." I sat down and tried to figure this out. "Ok. Marin, how far along is this?"

Lyra started to answer. "Nope. I've heard everything I want to hear from you right now. Marin?"

"It's about twenty weeks, it looks. It's incredible. About sixteen centimeters.

Kalista was thoroughly creeped out. "Jesus."

"Have you ever seen anything like this before?"

"No. and it's past the point where it could be anything but a human baby. With your DNA."

"Twenty weeks, not a clone."

"Technically it is a clone, but not made in any way we are familiar with. And we have a dilemma."

"Oh, yes, tell me the dilemma."

Marin looked around.

"There is a bump at about twenty weeks gestational. It's the start of a significant growth spurt. This is about sixteen centimeters- twenty weeks old."

Rojas took the bait, "So how big is a twenty one week old Fetus?"

"About twenty six centimeters. Maybe twenty seven."

I looked closely at it.

Dae read my mind. "It's already bigger than it was."

Marin interjected, "at this point, the fetus has fingerprints."

"Wait. MY fingerprints?"

"No. fingerprints are made environmentally. It would be an incredible coincidence if the fingerprints were even close to yours."

Kalista let out a deep breath. "So what do you want to do?"

I was keenly aware of the fact that I needed to make some decisions. And I needed to do it now.

"Ok. Marin, you watch this very closely. Take whatever space you need in the lounge and use it as a lab. Keep it contained. At this rate, it may die of old age before we land. Ro, grab your stuff. "

"I want you to take over Lyra's pod and figure out what the fuck is going on in there. Kal, help Lyra move her stuff in Roja's pod and then lock the door from the outside"

"Wait, what?"

"For your own good, you are on house arrest. We'll check in on you and Marin will get you some meds for this fever. Ro. Dae and I will help you clean up in Lyra's old pod so you can get settled. But figuring out what's going on is a priority. Everyone clear?"

Even Lyra followed up "yes, captain."

"Ok, let's do it."

"Wait," Kalista remembered. "What were you going to say, before? The crazy thing?"

"Oh, jeez. Ok. This is going to sound insane. So, we're in an Alcubierre bubble. It's job is to compress spacetime in front of us and expand it behind us. That's what powers the bubble to transport us. Is there any chance…And possible way… and i honestly don't know how this might work… where the space inside this ship is expanding?"

No one said anything.

Dae spoke first. "I don't even know how to think about that. Are we talking about some kind of non-Euclidean expansion?"

"Something is happening with the space in this ship. My pod is bigger than it should be. Lyra's pod is way bigger. There is a storage area where there should be none. "

"That is nuts." Rojas was trying to figure something out, clearly.

"Thanks, Ro."

"Actually, I didn't mean the idea was nuts. I wanted to say something before, but since we're all throwing it out there. When I tried to latch the tether on the first run near the rim of that door?"

"Yes, I remember" he looked more serious than I'd seen Ro look before.

"It crumbled. It broke. I remember thinking that it looked like metal in a thermocline."

Dae looked fascinated, "so what happens to metal when it's between two temperatures, a very cold and a very hot temperature."

"It reminded me of what you said about the membrane of the bubble around us. Between stationary movement and FTL."

Kalista interjected, "what two states do you think that the coupling was between? What was the thermocline?"

"I'm only saying this because Zed said the stupid thing first."

"Ok, thank you."

"What if the space inside the ship were expanding and the space it took up outside were not. What would happen to an object that sort of spent too much time in that in between space."

"Do you think something like that is possible?"

Dae took a breath. "Well. Space - the way it stretches - is a curvature. And principally that curvature of space is a function of gravity. I mean, technically it IS gravity. If you were able to build a giant wall around a black hole, for example, there would be more space inside that wall than the space that could be measured from outside the wall. This basically is true for any great curvature of space. It becomes measurable on a large scale. So if we built a box around the earth, we would see that the inside was bigger by a very small amount than the outside."

"So it's possible for a box to be bigger on the inside than the outside."

"Yes, but because of the way the well works, it's gradual. Incremental. There is no thermocline."

I stood up. "Ok. For Euclid's sake, let's table that and get what we can get done now. Dae, Ro, I'll meet you in the big room."

I put my arm on Marin's arm and nodded at him. The rest of the team left.

"Marin, if that WERE a clone, what would we be doing?"

"Oh. Well. It wouldn't be growing like this without a nutrient bath and an accelerator, for sure."

"I thought clones could be grown in a couple days."

"Sure. but it takes a lot. And the energy needed is significant. I don't know where this is getting nutrients or energy to grow"

"And once it's grown?"

"Well, we would implant memories and, well, give it clothes and an ID and send it on its way."

"Just do me a favor and really watch this thing."

"Ok."

By the time I had gotten to Lyra's old pod, Ro had gotten the lights working. In the light it was even more dramatic.

"Jesus. This is huge."

"Yeah, I don't understand this, at all. It's not even the same shape as the other pods."

I looked at Rojas, "So your pod is just a normal pod? 4 by 5?"

"Yep. I mean, it's configured just like yours, too. Desk next to the bed, multi in front of the bed. Regular size"

"Do you mind moving? I know this is kind of creepy."

"Do I mean taking the big room, mom? No, it's all good. I want to get good measurements and compare this against specs."

Dae and I pulled the bedding off and tossed it in the chute in the port corridor linking the pods to the Den. "I don't remember any of this in the original specs. Are the design specs for this ship changing?"

Dae looked up, "That's just a computer program, that would be the easiest thing to change. But who? And Why?"

Rojas was sweeping up into a dustpan. "So, even if we absolutely had to, we couldn't talk to Earth until this sprint is over? Because they would have the original specs."

Dae sighed. "No, we're completely cut off. While we're in the warp bubble, we're not really even in the same time frame as Earth. Our universes are incompatible. "

"That's a fucked up way of saying that."

"I know. It felt weird."

"We have to survive this for thirteen more days, and I think we can. But i'd like to figure it out and stop it."

"You're going to hate this, but I need to get out again and measure the outside of this ship."

"No way. No more walks."

Dae grabbed my arm. "This sucks but he's right. We've got ten meters or so of space all around us in this bubble. If there is any increase to the size of the outside of this ship, we need to know now. If any part of this ship intersects with the bubble in any way it'll slice it apart faster than we can even see."

"I hate this idea. Ro? I think it needs to be me. I don't want you out there again."

"This is my ship to maintain. And I know how to measure it and check it for anomalies."

"Fuck." I honestly hated the fact that he was right.

"Hey, guys." Dae called out from across the room. She had been moving the Multi to clean behind it. And was staring at the wall toward the floor.

Ro and i stepped over and saw what she was looking at.

"Am I crazy or is this a door?"

-12 Days

Cloning had become a relatively commonplace thing by 2150 but it was tightly regulated. With over ten billion people on the planet, there was no big rush to add more without purpose or reason. In some situations, people would agree to be cloned so that their special skills could be used in remote places. We knew what to do with clones. We knew how to manage the ethical implications, the technological implications, all of it.

We knew how to deal with clones.

I had no idea how to deal with this.

Marin was right. There was a significant leap in development between 20 and 21 weeks and this thing had grown nearly ten centimeters in one night.

And it was still growing.

"Can we figure out what is happening?"

Marin looked uncomfortable, "I'm at a loss. The development speed seems irregular. Milestones, however, are occurring in order. It's clearly healthy. All this is happening without an accelerator."

"What do you think is going to happen when it becomes viable?"

"Oh, it's already viable. Technically. It doesn't need any nutrients, energy, containment, shelter. I suspect I could just pour this container out on the floor and it would keep growing."

Dae was staring. "It really looks like you, already."

"Well, all of that's certainly not creepy at all." I sat down and tried to process all of this.

I could see Marin trying to spin this the best way he could. "Best case scenario, it's healthy and it's growth slows down at maturity, we overlay your identity on it and you have a clone to help with the mission. Two of you."

Dae shrugged, "All joking aside, that sounds fine. We could use the help."

I looked at Ro, "Worst case scenario?"

And he was ready, "It's a monster that eats all of our heads and shits them out onto Proxima Centuri B"

Kalista nodded, "Well, I'm confident it's somewhere in there- those two extremes."

"So we would overlay my memories and brain patterns on it?"

"Yes, that's not hard."

"From my brain?"

"Well, yes. We haven't managed to store brain waves and memories in anything but a brain, yet, long term. For a few hours, maybe."

"What happens if the clone grows on the ship for the next twelve days and makes some of its own memories?"

"Not a problem. The Human brain can contain a lot."

I looked at Marin and the light seemed to shrink, creating almost a tunnel between us. I tried to open my mouth and answer and, for a second, I couldn't.

"Captain?"

Dae shook my arm, "Zoo, are you ok?"

"Sorry. I'm sorry. This is really weird for me. I need to get past it. It's not normal, but it's just a clone, really, right?"

Marin nodded.

I stood up, "Beyond that, we are now looking for solutions that don't require another EVA. That's off the table. I need one of those famous 'work smarter - not harder' solutions. Anyone?"

Dae clarified, "To figure out if the outside of the ship is growing?"

"Yep. It just sounds crazy when I say it like that, so…"

"I can get out there and use a light tape to measure the distance to the bubble edge, without letting go of the ship at all." Ro was determined to do this.

"No. I know we can find another way."

Kalista thought out loud, "If we had light tapes attached to the exterior of the ship already we could do it from the comfort of the den."

"Do we have any light sources we could use that ARE attached?" I directed to Dae.

"Not really. We have nothing coherent, just, relly ambient light. And we can't focus them enough to make a difference. We have coherent impulse jets all over, but they won't tell us where the bubble edge is and I'm reluctant to use them. I don't want to shift us around in the bubble."

Ro stepped up, "We could be really old school and shoot tethers out from both sides. They would be sheared by the bubble edge and then we could retract them and determine how long they were now."

Kalista nodded, "That IS super old school but it would tell us laterally if the ship was getting bigger…"

"But we still have no way to tell bow to stern." I finished.

Marin looked up, "you guys said there was an atmosphere in the bubble?"

"Yes, but it's not breathable or anything. It's just not a vacuum." Dae brightened up, "And that's your point, isn't it?"

Kalista looked excited, "So we could potentially take a sample of the bubble atmosphere and then vent a pure gas into it while pulling an equal amount of gas. Then, wait a bit and resample and see how it disperses."

"So, Argon, maybe, it's non flammable, it's inert, it's harmless out there." Dae continued, "We have a supply in the welding bed we could vent outside, into the bubble. And then..."

Even Ro liked this idea, "We measure the diffusion."

This sounded perfect to me, "ok, that way we can figure out if the volume of the space around us between ship to bubble has changed at all without putting anyone in danger. I love it."

"And all it costs us is a little inert gas," Kalista finished.

"Great. Ro, how is it going mapping the newest specs for the ship?

"That's something I wanted to talk to you about, Captain," he pulled me aside. "Maybe you and I should take a look at this."

In Lyra's old pod, it was clear that Ro had moved in. His stuff was scattered all over and the room was now bright and cool, where before it was dark and musky hot.

"It seems about the same size as it was. That's good, right?"

"Yes, and I was hoping that it didn't actually grow or anything. I don't have any solutions for that. But that's not what I wanted you to see." He led me over to the area near the far corner of the pod. Here is where we had found before what looked to be a small door.

Which was now appreciably bigger.

"Oh, fuck me, You could have led with this."

"I don't get it, Captain, I've been trying to figure it out. I don't have any answers."

The door was about half a meter wide by a meter tall. It was flush with the floor and the far wall, as though the expansion of the room had revealed it. It was white, like the wall itself, with a metallic rim running all around it. We might have missed it or thought it was ornamental if we hadn't been looking at all of this so hard. It was clearly a door. And it was clearly bigger.

"Did you see it increase in size?"

"No, it was just bigger this morning. I've been measuring the room every few hours. I woke up and it was like this."

"Did you see it on the specs?"

"No. it's not there. I'm trying to make updates to the specs as we move along. Look at this." He held a tablet out and showed me the layout of the ship in blue. His fingers rested on a red slider and I could see the redline overlay of the new configuration. The new storage area, This update to Lyra's pod, my pod increases and one or two smaller adjustments."

"What are these?"

"I found these two this morning. This is near the back storage area and this one here is in the Den, right behind the clone."

"This doesn't feel like a coincidence to me." I could see him stealing glances at the door. He seemed fixated on it. "Are you ok, Ro?"

"Yeah, I just... It seems like it's moving, out of the corner of my eye."

I looked more closely as he stepped over to it.

"I think we should stay away from that. It could just be a stress point on the ship."

"It's perfectly made. The lines are perfectly machined. There is no way it can be accidental."

He reached toward it. I moved toward him, "Hey. cut it out. Leave that alone."

"I just,,," he looked at me and his eyes went dead. He lifted his arm and pushed the door. There was a click as seemingly magnetic fasteners opened. The door swung open outward and he fell into it, with his arm sinking into the space up to the shoulder. For just a second, there was a rush of vacuum and pressure that pulled me off my feet. I fell to my knees and started pulling myself toward Ro. He slid to the floor as the door swatch shut. In my head, I wondered how that could have happened with his arm in the way of the door, until I looked down.

His arm was completely missing. "Ro!" he was in shock, his eyes glazed over. I tried to cover him but the danger was over. The door was magically shut again. I felt for the area right below his shoulder where I could apply pressure to stop the blood, but the area was warm and sleek, covered in a thin layer of what seemed like sweat.

But no blood.

I carried him to the Medbay behind the Den, calling for Marin to meet me there. I had Kalista bring Lyra.

Marin administered something quickly to manage the pain. I looked down at where the arm was severed. I had never seen anything like it.

"Marin, why is there no blood here?"

"I don't know. This is definitely unusual. Did you see what removed the arm?"

"No, it looked like it was just sheared off as he fell into the door."

Kalista was confused, "That is not at all what would have happened if the door had opened to the hull of the ship. "

I knew that. It's more like what would have happened if it had opened to space outside the bubble. But that wasn't possible.

Lyra was collecting samples at the stub, where the arm came off. It looked smooth there, almost like new skin.

"This is insane. There is a growth of skin over the area. That's not possible. No blood, not damage to the tissues."

"What could have done that?"

"Nothing. Nothing I know of would have results in this. In a way, it looks like he was born without an arm."

"What's this slick stuff?"

Lyra closed her eyes to think. She knew that this was impossible.

"These are undifferentiated cells. Similar to the cells we found for that clone."

I stepped back. None of this was making sense. Was that door right up on the bubble? That meant the ship was in serious trouble.

"Kal, Dae, I need you guys to start that experiment right away. We need to see if the exterior of the ship has grown too close to the bubble."

"On it, Captain," Kalista rushed off with Dae right behind her.

"Lyra, is he going to be ok?"

"As far as I can see, Captain, his body is managing this well. He may be shocky, but I'm not even sure he's in that much pain."

"Can he hear me?"

"I believe so. He seems to be almost in a trance. But his blood pressure is stable now. He lost almost no blood but we've cycled a bunch through."

"Ro, talk to me, what happened? Why did you do that?"

He looked up at me. I don't know, Zed. I just wanted... I wanted to touch it."

"Were you trying to hurt yourself?"

"No, no, I just...wanted to feel it. Like something came over me. Part of me just wanted to go through the door."

"I'm blocking that pod off. This is insane."

"I'm sorry, Captain."

"It's ok. Get some rest." I looked up at Lyra and Marin, "Can he get something to sleep for a bit?"

"Sure, of course."

"Fuck. I'm going to the Den. Stay with him and keep me apprised. I need to see what's going on with the ship."

Lyra looked at me apologetically, "Aye, Captain."

"Ok, guys, I'm starting to panic a bit, not gonna lie," As I walked into the Den, Dae and Kal were positioned at two different screens.

"We're about to take a new sample. We released the argon and it should have had time to circulate." Kal stepped back from her monitor.

"We're measuring something we have no way to fix if it's off. That scares me, automatically," I leaned in.

Dae was sympathetic. I could see her furiously working out the math. "All right. First pass, the argon looks like it diffused evenly. And from the sample we got here it looks like the volume stayed steady. That means that the ship has not increased in size."

"What if the bubble increased in size along with a shipwide increase?"

"Leading to the exact same volume of space between the two? That is crazy unlikely. Besides, in transit like this we literally have no way to increase the bubble. That would have to be done back on earth."

"So, look at this." I took the tablet and sent it to the main monitor. The blue lines outlining the main spec were what Ro had charted. The red ones were the new ones.

The three of us looked at it. Many lines were identical, leading to a purplish sort of tone. But in some cases, the red lines expanded far beyond the blue ones. I did the math in my head, just as I knew the other two were.

"The ship is almost sixty cubic meters larger inside than it was when we left a few days ago."

Kalista flipped back and forth, "This isn't possible at all."

Dae posted the results of their experiment on the main monitor. "And the volume on the outside, the space between the edge of the bubble and the Ship's hull is exactly the same."

I sat down. "We have no choice but to accept that this ship is now bigger on the inside than the outside."

Dae was trying to figure it out desperately, "ok, right now, today, this is longest that any ship has been subjected to the Alcubierre metric. This ship has been under warp for about thirty hours longer than any ship before."

"What does that mean? Do we not understand how the gravity well works?" Kalista wasn't buying it. "And can a warp bubble create a doorway that opens to somewhere else?"

"If we think about it, we're traveling at all because we bent spacetime. So any additional space time bending and deformation within that artifact shouldn't be something we can't figure out." Dae really wanted this to have a sensible solution.

I wasn't so sure.

"Have we seen any other doors or weird pieces of construction?" Kal peered through the specs.

"We have a slight bulge at the back of the den and we have that storage area."

"Which, for all we know, is now bigger."

"Here's a dumb question, at what point do we worry that life support systems can't manage the larger space?"

Dae was suddenly back in her element, "Oh, that isn't a problem at all. We could be out for months with the amount of oxygen we have. And there is more than enough energy to heat the space. We have other concerns, though."

"Ok, like what concerns?"

Dae thought for a second. "Come here."

The three of us walked to the back of the den. We could see the clone floating in the tank. It was larger now, almost a viable looking baby. I peered closer. It really did look like me.

Dae bent down and pulled the tank aside. The liquid in it sloshed a bit then settled. Behind the tank we could see a bulge- slightly rounded, of an extra meter or so of space. It looked like a nook that someone had built to install a bookshelf. But it looked more organic than the door or storage space. It curved.

Dae pointed, "This here. This is the bulge that Ro identified. Behind this area is the Medbay. We were just there, so you all probably saw it doesn't show up there."

"That's right." I leaned in and knocked on the wall. "This area here would be right behind the patient monitor for the first bed. Ro is in it. There is no bulge outward on that side."

"So, we have some non-euclidian shit happening here," Kal folded her arms.

But Dae had another point to make.

"This wall is important. I mean, most of these walls are important. Every wall in a ship this size is essentially a retaining wall - every wall is meant to add to the structural stability of the ship. I would not have built this like this. It's not a sound shape. Stress on top of this bulge may push down and compact the space. Or it would if this were a normal ship doing normal things."

"And…" I could tell there was more. I know Dae like the back of my hand now.

"And what the hell is this extra material made out of? I can tell you what the ship is made of, what wires are behind every wall, what is happening behind that space or that one. I have no idea what is in this. The giant expanse of Lyra's old room? I have no clue what any of that is made of or how it functions."

"It's the same materials, though, right?"

"I have no idea. I literally have no clue."

This seemed to hit Kalista kind of hard. She was a hard science person. And she trusted things like Nasa-built ships.

Because they were built according to rigid rules.

The idea that this ship had gone all wild wild west was affecting her.

She stepped back and I tried to grab her. She fell into the cylinder for the clone and it toppled over and smashed to the ground, liquid spraying everywhere. She scrambled and slipped to the floor.

The clone slid across the room on a wave of thick liquid across the floor. Dae checked Kal and they both seemed fine so I turned my attention to the clone. It had slipped behind a chair near the front of the lounge area. I pulled the chair back and looked down.

It looked almost as though it were sleeping, propped up against the wall, covered in slime. I reached down for it when it opened its eyes and looked right at me. In a tiny whisper, it said:

"You fucked up."

-11 Days

"I know we don't really know each other, but I've heard a lot of great things about you," The doctor tried to fill time while I was in the medical bed for my checkup. She was petite, a redhead with a kind face. She seemed quick and smart but her demeanor was more like a nurse than a doctor.

She listened.

"I heard that you are a great captain, a really good person to be on a team with." she pulled the thermometer out of my mouth, letting me speak. Her name was Lyra Tambor, I believed. From what I had heard, her father was a bigwig at the state department so she had used her mother's maiden name so as to advance on her own. I respected that.

"That's nice to hear, I admit. I've heard good things about you, too. I kept my eyes trained on the ceiling. I wasn't about to do anything that would impact this mission.

I needed this.

"And you seem to be in pretty ridiculously good health." She looked up at the monitor over the bed.

I could feel all the leads across my skin, machines making their own assessments of me, trying to determine if I was acceptable for this trip. "I am. I have always been."

"I know you've been through some hard times lately. Is there anything you want to talk about?"

This was a troubling crossroads. NASA knew about everything that had been going on with me. And they knew I had spoken to therapists and specialists. Was it more healthy and normal to say I needed to talk or was it better to say I had talked it out?

"I appreciate that, Lyra, is it?"

"Yes. I'm here if you need."

I took her hand. "It has been a year, for sure. And I can't tell you how much I appreciate all you doctors for all the talk. I feel like it worked."

"That's good. That's really good. How do you feel about leaving earth?"

I leaned back, "Just between you and me, maybe some space would be good right now, you know? Just a place where you can be a little more alone sometimes."

"I hear that. The crowds seem to get denser every day."

"I'm excited about going to make a life for some of those people." I looked up at her, "Besides, we're certainly going to get to know each other soon."

She laughed, "Oh, yes. I guess so."

"How do you feel about that?"

"I confess, it's a very strange feeling. But I'm glad to be of service."

"That's exactly how I feel." I closed my eyes. I hoped that this conversation had mitigated her fears. The last thing I needed right now was to be held back.

"Everything checks out."

"I appreciate you, doc." I tried to see if I could stop thinking for five minutes.

She whispered to me. "In a way, I wish I could come with you."

I opened my eyes and looked up at her. She seemed so kind. I liked her.

"In a way, you are."

She laughed and picked up her clipboard.

"You can get dressed and let yourself out anytime. Talk to you soon, Captain Kimura."

"Thanks, doc."

"So what did I hear?" The clone was in bed two of the medbay while Ro was sleeping in bed one. I stared into the slight white face of the doctor, framed with the mop of reddish hair.

"I'm not sure. But this clone is not capable of speaking yet." She looked confused. Marin stood next to her and agreed.

"It has no overlays and hasn't learned any language. I'm not even sure the larynx is developed enough. It's just not possible.

De and Kalista were too far away to hear the whisper. But I was 100% sure that this clone spoke to me.

Lyra looked at marin. I knew she felt like she was still in trouble and was likely unwilling to oppose me. But they looked certain.

"Hey, I believe you," called out Ro from the other bed.

Dae and Kal were flanking Ro's bed. Dae offered up, "and he's only a little crazy."

"I hate all of you. Even little baby clone me."

"I heard the experiment went well?" Ro was clearly interested in our findings about the size of the ship.

"Yep. The outside of the ship seems like it's the same size. As soon as you are feeling better, though, I need you to keep up on what's happening inside. We have eleven more days."

"I'm feeling fine." It doesn't even hurt.

Marin added, "well, I'm guessing it hurts, but the combination of extreme manliness and pain medication is managing it."

"Extreme. Thank you." Ro laughed.

"Are we going to be able to grow a new arm for lefty over there?"

Marin seemed kind of excited, "Oh, yeah. Once we're planetside, there is a ton of gear sent via unmanned nanoships. There's just no one there to run it yet. We can handle that. But take a look at this."

Marin moved over to Ro's bed and called me over. He pulled off the covering for the wound. It looked clean, with a thin film over it - a familiar one.

"Is that what I think it is?"

"Yes, it's undifferentiated cells. Very similar to what grew that clone over there. Coded to Rojas. And they are already building him what looks like a new arm."

"And we don't know why or how?"

"No, we do not. It goes on the list of things we don't understand. This cut is unlike anything I've ever seen, too. All of it is just a big question mark."

"Well, I can't tell you how much I hate that. " I addressed the room. "Ok, That pod that Ro was in, the big one... we board that up. No one goes in there. That's done. Ro, you move into my pod."

"Where are you going to go?"

"I'm getting a space u-haul and moving in with my girlfriend. Is that ok, Dae"

She smiled and nodded.

For the next eleven days, we're staying away from strange doors, we're staying in the ship, we're keeping a close eye on clones, we're going to try to have a few very uneventful days in a row. Any area that may be bulging or distressed through expansion, we leave alone. If a game room appears, we stay out of it. Is that all clear?"

A round of "Yes, Captain" rang out.

"Lyra, Kal, I need to talk to you."

The three of us stepped into the starboard corridor. "Ok, Lyra, I'm still a bit pissed at you, but you are the doctor here, and at the end of the day, I trust you. Kal, you are my oldest friend in the world and I need to run something past you both. "

Lyra looked back and forth and nodded.

"I've been having dreams that are sometimes presenting as memories. There are three of them I need to run past you two right now. Is that cool?"

Kal put her hand on my arm, "Of course."

"First up, Lyra. I remembered you giving me a physical before this mission. You and I talked. You said you wished you could come. I said that you were coming, in a way. What was that about?"

"Could that have been someone else?"

"No. I am 100% sure it was you."

Lyra looked pained, "I didn't examine anyone before this mission. I joined the program, went through all the steps, and then ended up here. It was a whirlwind. I don't remember too much of it, even. But I was not the doctor examining people for the mission."

"This seems really real. Kal. who examined you for the mission?"

Kalista looked up. She seemed to be searching her memory.

"I honestly do not remember. I joined up, and like she said, everything happened so fast. I don't know."

"What could it have meant that you were coming, 'in a way'?"

"I don't know. I'm clearly here. I mean, I came with."

"So you don't remember having a conversation with me during my checkup?"

"No. I don't."

"Kal, we talked about the girl in the pool, do you remember that?"

"Yeah, in Mexico, I remember."

"Do you know what I keep thinking about it?"

Kalista was unsure, "I don't know. I mean, it was horrible, but..."

Lyra offered, "Well, what if the idea of being trapped, starved for air, dying in front of people who can't save you, was like a trigger?"

"For what?"

"What does it sound like? Dying in front of the whole world suffocating, trapped in a small space?"

"It's dying in a space ship."

"I think so."

Kal perked up, "Do you think that's why it resonates like that, why you can't let go?"

"Maybe. I don't know."

"What's the third?"

"A memory of having something implanted in my head. A tiny box, maybe?"

"A box? I don't know anything about that."

"Something is gnawing at me, making me think I can figure all this out."

"If you can, more power to you." Kalista was clearly frustrated. "None of this is making any sense. I keep falling back on the idea that this is a long time to be under warp. We're deforming our personal universe in some way. Maybe your dreams are trying to tell you that something isn't going right?"

Lyra looked up, "What if we just stop and pause the trip for a little bit?"

"I wish we could. We have the ability on the ship to turn off the warp bubble, but not to initiate it. If we stop, we are stuck, as far from home as any person has ever been in history."

Dae poked her head out of the medlab. "Hey, guys, you need to come in here."

The clone was sitting up in the bed, looking around the room. At this point, it looked like a six month old baby.

Marin had brought some clothes he had modified. "I want to just make sure she's not flopping around here naked."

"I appreciate that. How fast is this?"

He looked at me, "This is exponential. And there is no accelerator. It's a jerky development so i don't think I can gauge how fast. But she'll be ready for an overlay very soon. Before we get planetside.

"In the meantime, we need to take care of her, right?"

"I can keep an eye on her. I used to babysit my little brothers and sisters. I'm totally equipped, Captain."

"Are you sure you want to take this on?"

"No problem. I can be primary for now and if anyone wants to help, they can, here and there. I can move my stuff in here and stay here as soon as Ro moves into your old pod."

"Marin, I appreciate it, but let me know if it gets to be too much, ok?"

"I got it, no worries."

"Any more…. Talking?"

"No. none."

"Ok, everyone, I meant what I said about uneventful. Let's aim for that, ok? I'll meet you guys in an hour or so for dinner."

Dae placed the doll into a box. I confess I was nervous having anyone touch it, even her.

"I'm not going to break it." She grabbed me around the waist.

"I know. It's just. You know. It matters."

"Well, I appreciate that. I do"

"I really don't have a lot of stuff. But are you sure this is ok?"

"Oh, captain, my captain. It's good. Are you getting cold feet?"

"No way. I said i love you first, you know?"

"Well, that's not how I remember it. You were pretty shy. I had my hands all over you when we first met"

"Ok, I do remember that."

"Did I need to put my hand on your back while showing you around?

Probably not."

"Clearly you did."

Dae looked up at me and moved my hair away from my face, like she does when she has something serious to say.

"You're having strange dreams and it's freaking you out."

"I really think it's just the fallout from what is happening here. I'm very confused and I think my brain is working overtime. If you put on your scientist hat, what do you think it happening?"

Dae sat on the bed, "well, first of all, I never take my scientist hat off. That's my main hat. Second, yeah, I'm worried. There are seventeen thousand people who've been asleep for about nineteen years about to land on a planet that they think is being prepared for them. We need to be there to wake them up, to help get everything going. We need to be there. And i know that's all you're thinking about right now. What happens, though, if this kind of travel has safety issues for trips of this length? What happens if somehow, reality is being warped?"

"Yeah, that's everything in my head right now. But what if it's not reality being warped. What if it's our brains being affected? I remember some things that may not have happened. And don't remember some other things."

"Like what?"

"So." I sat down next to her, "Who did your physical for this trip? You had to have one, right?"

"I don't think I did. I remember you said I was coming. And they deferred. My lasst physical was less than a year ago, so they said fine."

"Does that sound right to you?"

"I don't know. When i think about it too hard I start to get that feeling again, like i don't belong here."

"You belong here as much as I do. But I am just starting to get worried that my brain isn't working perfectly. Which would be a disaster."

"Does it seem to you like all of us have been a bit 'off'?"

"What do you mean?" I was feeling it but I wasn't sure why.

"I don't know Lyra well, but she behaved strangely. She lied and told you she destroyed those cells. And Marin just took her word for it? We were all ok with Ro going EVA just to inspect that room? And what did he do with that door?"

"Right. And, I feel like I just stood there and let him put his arm out that door."

"All of us have just shrugged and accepted this clone out of nowhere. Marin dressed it up and is taking care of it like a baby. I mean, it is a baby, but..."

"No, you're right. We just accepted it. I could have thrown it out. I should have, maybe?"

"Now that it's sitting up, she's sitting up. What can we do?"

"I don't know. I'll tell you this, the next eleven days can't go by fast enough for me."

Ro was setting the table when we stepped into the den.

"What the hell, man?"

"I'm fine. The Doctor gave me a clean bill of health."

"Well, we'll all go grab the rest of your stuff out of that room after dinner. My pod is cleared out."

"Awesome. I'm just going to move every day or two until we get there."

"There will be a nice stable room for you on B, trust me."

Kal spoke up, "Speaking of which, once we plant there, we'll get to say we colonized it. So we'll be free to name it."

"I want to remind you guys that there is not currently a planet named Acostaworld."

Dae laughed, "We'll keep that in mind."

"Not, you, doofus, Kedi is the captain." Kal looked at me, "What do you want to name it?"

"I just want to get there. Safely. At that point, I don't care what it's named."

"I suggest 'Motown'"

Dae seemed to like that, "a rich history."

"Exactly, what do you say, Captain?"

"Acostaworld is still available."

"Let's table this discussion until we plant something. Then we're figure out what to put on the return address stamp. Where are Marin and Lyra?"

Ro and Kal looked at each other, "They are making sure the clothes for the baby fit."

"I thought they had clothes already." I was not prepared for this. There was a kid on this ship now. And it was me. That was certainly creepy.

Ro dropped a plate and grabbed it out of the air.

"nice catch, cowboy" Kal patted him on the back.

I walked over to him, "Ro. You're right handed, right?"

"I was. I mean, I think I am."

"You seem to be doing a lot of stuff really easily with your left hand."

He looked at me. "Yeah, I can't explain it. Look."

He opened the drawer below the table and pulled out a tablet. Flipping it on, he started writing on it with his left hand. The writing was smooth and legible.

"I couldn't have done that a couple of days ago."

"So you're able to write with your left hand now?"

"Write, eat, everything. I don't understand. It's like my body just switched over. Like I'm left handed now."

"I looked at his hand. I put a fork in it. He held it as though he had been left handed his whole life.

"What do Lyra and Marin think about this?"

"I haven't brought it up. I don't understand what is happening but it feels normal. I'm not really feeling any pain, either, and I know the meds must have worn off."

"Not at all?"

"Not really, no."

Kalista took his hand, "I know that the brain often will use a different piece when one is damaged. Maybe it's just adjusting to this damage?"

"I don't think that's how it works. "

"Guys, I'm fine. Don't worry about me. It's all going to be ok."

I could hear the other two walking into the Den so I turned to ask them their medical opinion. I saw Marin and Lyra standing there holding hands with the clone who wore a small sack like dress. She looked to be about two years old and was standing on her own. She looked at me and her face brightened.

"Hi, Mommy."

-10 Days

I was fifteen years old when the Leviathan launched. It was an event that seemed to fascinate everyone on earth. It was the first of the large scale colony ships and it held seventeen thousand and fifty men and women, in suspended animation and virtually nothing else.

This was meant to be a ship of people, a giant box that just held souls.

It was a huge and boxy ship. It didn't need to be aerodynamic - it wasn't flying in the conventional sense. Not through the atmosphere. It just had to be sturdy.

In the twentieth century, they used to have black boxes in airplanes. The black boxes would contain the final communication made into our out of the plane. It would contain important information about the fate of the plane. And it was designed to survive anything that might destroy the plane.

It was very dense and strong.

Comedians at the time used to joke, "hey, why not just make the whole plane out of the material used for the black box." it was funny and it pointed out that this thing that only contained information, would be safe while real people died.

But that was impossible. The materials used to make the black box were dense and strong and heavy. An entire plane made from this would never fly. It would just sit there, dead, on the tarmac.

Space exploration let us upend considerations like that. All of Leviathan was built from the materials you might have used to build a black box. It was sturdy and thick and the hull was difficult to penetrate. In a way, it was a vault full of people, protecting them from nearly anything that might happen. These people would represent Earth.

And they were already taking a massive risk.

This ship was sent first, Giant and heavy, with its relatively slow, methodical, but reliable Fuchs-Minkowski subluminal drive. It would travel at about 20% of the speed of light and would take nearly twenty years to reach its destination.

Inside, many of these people were just average people. They didn't have unique skills that would enable them to live on a colonized world. They were volunteers, people who had had enough of life on a thickly populated aggressive planet and were looking for something different.

Not long after they left, nanoships would be sent with supplies and resources that they could use in their new homes. These ships were unmanned and would make the trip in just a few years, landing on their own and, in some cases, beginning to build absent human intervention.

Later, NASA would send ships like ours to these colonized worlds, containing specialized knowledge and people prepared to ramp up the colony, to manage any problems that might happen at the start, and to prepare it for the wave of people that would live there.

These were ships with experimental drives that could make the trip in weeks- drives that could never work on the larger behemoths. And the makeup of these ships was still in flux, even as we left. What would be the smartest approach? How to send these specialized skills off world without depleting the homeworld?

The colonization process required we ask a lot of questions like that. How do we prioritize the lives of the colonizers without sacrificing the welfare of the people back home? As we spent trillions of dollars to manage this new period in human history, we asked ourselves that question a lot.

We explored the answers, worked hard to figure out all the angles and dynamics. We tried to find ways that would preserve life but also manage skills the most effective way we could. We worked.

And we experimented.

Anyone who has never spent the night having a conversation with their seemingly two year old clone will likely not understand how it feels to wake up the next day and have a series of conversations with that same clone, only now looking like she is approaching four. The clone was advancing nearly as quickly as she might have under an accelerator but was gaining milestones in ways that I'm assured a clone under these circumstances would not.

"So explain to me how she is picking up language so well." I addressed Marin over breakfast.

"You could just ask me, mommy."

"I know, sweetheart, I just want to hear what Marin thinks."

"Honestly, she knows more than I do at this point. Toddlers learn through a near insane amount of coordinated repetition. We don't realize how many times we need to say things before they are learned. But that doesn't seem to be the case here."

"What do we call her?"

"You can use my name, mommy"

That was new. She hadn't asserted that she had a name up until now.

"Ok, little one. Do you want to name yourself?"

"I already have a name, silly."

Marin looked at me and shrugged, this was the first he had heard of this, too.

"What is your name, then?"

"My name is Ersi."

Kal walked over and leaned in,"well, that's a pretty name, dear. I like it."

"Where did you hear that?"

"I didn't. It's just my name. Hey. What happened to his arm?" She pointed behind me at Ro.

He turned around and smiled. "Well, young lady, I think that's something we're all trying to figure out.

I looked at her. "That is the first question I've heard you ask. Is there anything you want to know?"

Ersi cocked her head a little, 'What is this place?"

Marin and I locked eyes, "Well, it's a ship. We're on our way to a new planet to get it ready for some people. "

"That sounds like fun"

"It will be fun. I hope."

"What's the ship called?"

"It's a Veda Ecko ship. Number six. But we're the first to launch. Do you like that name?"

"What does it stand for?"

That was curious. How could she have known that ECKO stood for something? That it wasn't just a name"

Dae leaned in, "Ersi, do you want to come play for a bit?"

Ersi nodded enthusiastically and the two of them moved off to the lounge.

At the arch she stopped and whispered to Dae. Dae looked at me. "Sweetheart, can you say that again to everyone?"

Erse looked right at me, as though she knew I was the one who needed to hear it.

"There should be more room. Here."

I looked around at everyone. "We have the room we have, sweety. Is that ok?"

Ersi nodded. "I think it has to be."

Dae stepped into the lounge with her.

I turned to Marin as Lyra came into the Den area.

"What the fuck was that?"

Kalista understood what I was thinking. "Space...Room... what if there is a connection here?"

"I have so many questions."

Marin looked more flustered than I had ever seen him. "I wish I had answers. I have more questions than you."

"Ok, let's hear them."

Marin thought. "Ok, She invented a name out of nowhere, using words she has never heard. Where did that come from?"

"Yeah, I don't know."

Lyra joined in, "She's conjugating verbs."

"Kids will do that, right?"

"Well, at first, they'll use the verb as a block, whatever you use. Then, at about four or five, she will start to take it apart and make conjugation mistakes. Then, eventually get them right on her own. This is... bizarre."

Marin nodded, "And 'already?' ... 'just? These are adverbs. That's unusual to start with. But had anyone here used the word 'already' before she just did?"

I thought back. Now I wish I had been keeping track.

"You're saying she is using words she couldn't possibly know?"

"She's definitely using words beyond her. The concepts needed to parse the idea of 'already' are deep. But adverbs? These show up last in the cognitive toolkit for kids."

"I was a precocious child. Does that matter?"

Lyra went into pediatric clinician mode, "It's not about being precocious. It's about pulling words and concepts from out of nowhere. We're literally feeding her almost nothing and she's thriving. In every way. She's not eating enough food, getting enough conversation, getting enough play, any of it, yet she is hitting milestones cognitively faster than physically. And you see how fast she's moving physically."

That concerned me. "Can we put some programs together to help manage her development the right way?"

"That's just it. She's basically raising herself. She doesn't seem to need anything."

"Is this accelerated development going to continue?"

Ro huffed, "if it does, she's going to die of old age before we get to B."

Marin shook his head, "I literally have no idea. There is nothing normal about this. And look at this."

He pulled Ro over and lifted the dressing on his arm.

"What is that?"

"It's what it looks like. His arm is beginning to grow back."

"Jesus. I thought we needed the facilities on the planet to do that"

"No, you don't get it. Lyra and i- we're not doing this. We're not growing it back. It's doing it on its own."

"The cells?"

"It looks that way. The undifferentiated cells."

"How does it feel?"

"Honestly, I feel good. It feels ok. And I'm not being macho. I feel fine."

"Good. Because I was going to ask for your help"

Ro, Kal, and I grabbed some equipment from storage and made our way down the aft halfway. Ro seemed on edge.

"We don't need to do this. I'm not going back in there, for sure."

"No one is. Think of this as kid proofing the ship."

Kal liked that, "we need to do more of that, honestly."

"Well, we start here. Look, something in that room cut your arm off. That's reason enough to block it off."

"I get that. I'm with you."

We moved down the corridor toward the offending pod.

"We'll block it off and then figure it all out after we land. I feel like landing and just walking around this ship is going to give us the answers we need."

Kal cocked her head, "I hope so."

Ro stopped, "Wait. Am I insane or…"

"Sonafabitch."

I put my hand on the wall in front of me. I tried closing my eyes and just feeling the wall in front of me. It was completely smooth.

The doorway to the pod was gone.

Dae and Marin were playing with Ersi in the Lounge area when we came back to the Den. I tried not to panic.

"Ro, can you pull up the internal cameras in pod three?"

"Got it. But…"

The monitor over his head was black.

Nothing.

"Are the cameras not responding?"

"According to the system, there are no cameras in pod three. There is no pod three."

"Fuck. Can you pull up the camera outside pod three?"

"Yes, I can. One sec." Now, on the monitor, was the smooth wall we had just encountered in the fore part of the port corridor.

"What just happened?"

Kalista was energized. This was taunting the scientist in her and she was growing into it, trying to meet this new universe we were experiencing.

"What if that pod knew we weren't going to use it anymore?"

"I don't know if I'm willing to go there yet."

"No, think about it for just a second. We were just on our way to block it off."

Ro sighed, "We need a better answer than that."

"Can you rewind? Can you show us what was happening in that pod before? Go back?"

Ro looked up at me, "that's the thing. These files here are all connected to their cameras. It's how we call them up. Pod three doesn't exist, so the computer is acting like it never existed. I can't call up the archived footage, either."

Kalista reached over to a terminal, "so it's gone?"

Ro closed his eyes to think. "Well, yes, and no."

"What does that mean?"

"The archival footage saves to the main archives every twenty minutes. It's indexed by time and not primarily by location. So if I access the main archives, I can see blocks of time, in twenty minute intervals. It will show main cameras and then we can zoom in on the one we want. Hypothetically"

"Ok, I like that, hypothetically. How do we do that?"

Ro opened a drawer to pull out a pad. He flicked the content onto the main monitor.

"We just finished a time block. This was two blocks ago. I can have it show all the cameras indexed as residential."

On the screen, you could see six squares, one for each pod.

"There it is. Pod three."

"Great," Ro seemed more on top of things now. This was making sense. "We know that it was here forty minutes ago."

"Nothing unusual."

"The light is on. Why would the light be on?" Kalista looked over.

"If you jump back to sixty minutes, is the light on?"

Ro moved his fingers on the pad and 6 other boxes filled the screen. Pod three was dark.

"Nope. The light is off."

"Can we see the most recent 20 minute block?"

"Give me about a minute. It's processing. Wait. we can view while it's processing. We just can't fast forward."

He flicked it onto the main monitor and we could see the room. The lights were on.

"So who turned the lights on?"

"So far, nothing. This is a little over twenty minutes ago."

"Ok. what do you guys see?"

Ro was squinting. "Is that a - a shadow?"

"Where?"

"Up to the left."

It looked like it might have been a dark splotch on the video. Until it moved. The big problem was that the cameras in the residential pods were really more of a troubleshooting afterthought. No one wanted to be constantly surveilling people in their rooms. They weren't set expertly, they didn't move or spin, and they weren't as aggressively placed as cameras elsewhere.

"What is happening?"

"It looks like someone might be in there- in the bathroom area. I can't access any sound."

It was incredibly frustrating not being able to move around or fast forward. We sat there and watched a blurry figure just out of range of the camera, only visible when the lightest of shadows fell against the far wall.

"This is insane. I told everyone to stay out of that pod."

Kalista looked up, "We were here. Right around that time. I don't understand."

The figure moved against the wall, right below the camera. We could see the shadow, but not the figure itself. Its movements were initially smooth then became more jerky."

"What is happening there?"

Ro shook his head, "It's not on the camera, The video is acting fine. However this is moving, it was actually moving."

I looked closely at the video. The door on the other side of the room was partially dark, up against the far darker wall. It looked bigger now, though, as though the wall had pulled away from it and let it expand. It was almost as though it was being revealed by the wall receding away. There was nothing else in the room except a few papers. The door began to vibrate a bit, shaking as though it was being pulled on from the other side."

"Look at that door."

The vibration became more intense and I could see it begin to bulge in and out a little. You had the sense it was being jimmied by a strong external force. The room began to vibrate a bit.

"We had no notification of any of this?"

"Nothing- the monitors didn't record any of this."

"No pressure changes in this ship?"

Ro was adamant, "Nothing. This should have set off a thousand alarms"

Then I saw it. A flash of red. Reddish hair.

"It's Lyra. Damn. Kal, call her, get her here now."

"Aye, Captain" Kal rushed out.

"What is she doing?"

The door vibrated harder and then, without warning, broke open outward, fueling a microstorm of papers and dirt all over the room, swirling and jostling to escape out of the open portal. You could almost see the shape of the wind as it swarmed over every piece of flotsam in that pod, pulling it outward.

Finally, we could see Lyra's shape, making her way around the room, hugging the walls tightly. Somehow, she was hanging on, not joining the mass eddy current of tiny junk flowing out into space. She was mostly in darkness.

She approached the camera. Pulling herself along the wall, she began to move below the camera. We lost her for a minute as she maneuvered below the camera, trying to stay close to the wall. It looked like she was grabbing something, retrieving something.

The camera shuddered as she grabbed onto it and we could see, on the sides, her fingers grabbing onto the camera itself. She pulled herself up, facing the door and we could see the mass of red hair, falling down over her shoulders."

What was she doing?

Kalista came running into the room, "She's gone."

"You can't raise her on radio?"

"And I can't find her anywhere. She's gone."

Ro turned, "Computer Locate Lyra Tambor"

A red light flicked on the side monitor.

"Computer. One more time. Lyra Tambor. Locate her position on the ship."

Another red light lit up.

On the screen, we could see the back of Lyra's head. She pulled back, away from the camera, letting her arms extend. And she turned.

Ro looked confused, "It says she's not on the ship."

And there it was, right where her face would have been filling nearly a third of the screen, her arms still holding on tightly to the camera, we saw it. The front of her head was smooth, featureless.

It looked like something had stolen her face.

I jumped as she let go of the camera on the screen, falling backwards into the door where her body compressed and contracted, folding like a piece of paper and slipping out the doorway.

The lights in the room dimmed and the walls seems to almost disappear until the screen was black

Completely black.

ECKOSPACE 6

-09 Days

"Where is Ersi?" I looked up at Marin as he came into the Den.

"I just got her down to sleep in the Medbay. She's fine."

"Ok, thanks, Ro, can we keep that on the monitor here- like a baby monitor for now?"

"Yep. Got it."

"I'm sorry to be keeping you guys up all night, but I highly doubt any of you would be sleeping anyway."

Kalista shivered, "Not me."

"How is the new map looking?"

Ro went first, "Well, I drilled that hole into the new storage space. It's stayed consistent. No volume change. The bulge at the back of the lounge is also the same. The Den and control areas are unchanged. The pod I'm staying in, however, your old pod, has expanded by another ten centimeters."

Marin read off a pad he had with him, "The medbay is about two meters wider than it was at launch. I feel like I just never noticed it. My pod has not really changed, I think. I measured it and it seems standard."

"My pod is the same size. No difference. But the port storage area is about a meter taller than it is in the specs. It's a lot, but if all of this weren't going on, who would have measured?" Dae shrugged. This was really getting to her. This ship was sort of her baby, in a way.

"Ok, Dae, is there anything happening right now or potentially happening that should make us worry about structural stability?"

"Well, Ro and I programmed the ship to run that argon diagnostic test every two hours and alert us to external changes. So far, there have been none. We're going to need to find another inert gas, soon, though, because soon the entire space will be full of argon."

"What else do we have, Xenon?"

"Too dense. Not enough of it."

Ro offered up, "Carbon Dioxide?"

Dae nodded, "Yep, that's probably our best bet. So get breathing, people."

"But nothing internally is a danger"

"I don't think so. Ro?"

"Yeah, I don't think that anything is a huge threat. But I wonder."

"What? Let's hear it."

"In all the electrical, computing, and lighting fixtures, there are terminals, poles, points where energy is meant to jump from place to place or through materials. I don't know what happens if those spaces get bigger. I mean, I don't know how any of this is working?"

"Can you run some tests on affected areas?"

"I was thinking I could do that."

"Sounds like a good idea. I'd rather know before something big and bad happens. How about you, kal, anything?"

"My pod seems to be the same size. I'm measuring everything I can. I'm researching any way i can, but my hands are tied a bit. We're totally cut off from all research materials on earth for another 9 days now."

"Yeah, we're sort of self contained until then. We have to remember that No matter what happens to us, Leviathan is going to land when it lands. If we're not there to accommodate them, they stay sleeping. This mission means something and even down a person, we need to make it work."

"Understood." Marin looked down, clearly sad.

"Marin, I know this is hard, but none of us really knew Lyra. You spent more time with her than any of us. Can you think of any reason why she might have done this?"

"I really can't. She was happy yesterday. She was in her element working with Ersi."

Looking up, I could see her on the monitor, sleeping. I wondered what was going through her head.

"This is going to sound dumb, but did she say anything to her?"

"You think that the clone might have pushed her to do it?"

"I really have no idea right now. At all. I'm open to anything."

Ro looked uncomfortable, "I looked at that video over and over again and what we saw wasn't a trick of the light."

"Until we know more, nobody is alone with the clone, ok?"

Marin looked at me, "I don't mind watching out for her. I am monitoring her growth."

"Ok, I'm going to crash in the medbay in another bed. We'll both be around her. Is that ok?"

"I'll set it up."

On the way out, I put my arms around Dae, "I'll come by in a few hours. I just don't want anyone to be alone with the clone right now."

"I get it. Be careful. I'm not going to be sleeping much. I have a concern I wanted to talk to you about, though."

"Ok, shoot."

"You know how the old planes used to have a black box flight recorder?"

"I was just thinking about that yesterday. Weird."

"Well, we're totally out of touch with Earth. If some of these things are happening because we've been under superluminal warp longer than anyone else, we need to be able to record and pass that information on. You know. In case."

I saw where she was going now. If we imploded or disappeared, Earth might never know about these effects. We needed to find a way to document this and pass it on.

But how?

"Can you think of a way that we can get information back to Earth if anything happens to us?"

"I'm wracking my brain now and I can't imagine. But there has to be a way, right?"

"Do you think these effects didn't happen to the nanoships under superluminal warp?"

"They would have known, right? Unless it was harmless and the ships' computers didn't care."

If it didn't happen to them and it's happening here, what is different?"

"Well, we're in a manned ship."

"Ok, so what are the chances all of this is an illusion, happening in our heads?"

"The chances? To be honest, I think they're good."

That took me aback a bit. "So we don't believe what we see?"

"I don't know. I don't know what to believe."

"Believe me. I'll come see you soon." I kissed her.

I looked up and I was staring almost directly into the sun. I could feel my sunglasses on my head so I slipped them down over my eyes. I reached up to pull off the big hat that had been shading me.

There was something different this time.

I heard a crash. I looked down and saw that the drink had fallen out of my hand. Did that happen first?

Or was it this?

The alarm went off. I'm sitting up now. I'm not the only one who hears it.

People are rushing around, all around me. They are rushing toward it,

And the scream. That's what's different this time. I know what's happening before i get there. The scream sounds familiar.

It's so familiar.

I run toward it, pushing people aside. I'm plowing through them, elbowing them out of the way.

Now I'm trying to listen and gauge where I'm going. But I've done this before. I know where it's at, right? I see the pool up ahead, surrounded by people. There is a sign. A number six enclosed in a circle. Pool six.

So many people. There is a man in front of me and I have to almost punch him to move him out of my way. And I see it.

Before I see the girl, I see the clear plastic closure moving inexorably to my left. I kneel at the edge of the pool and try to hold it. I did my feet into the cement at the side of the pool and pull as hard as I can with both hands. The poly enclosure digs into my hands without a single ounce of give. I feel the blood form in my palms as it cuts through the thin skin of my palms.

I want to jump into the pool and push, but there is no way. Even if I could gain traction on the bottom, the pressure is unyielding. If twenty of us had been trying to stop it, it would have cut us all to ribbons.

I yell out, looking for the machinery that is meant to stop this but i don't see anything.

Except her.

I see her black hair weaving out around her like a spiderweb as she desperately tries to race the enclosure to the other side. She's too far. She'll never make it. Her fists beat at the pool covering, just millimeters above the surface of the water. She's already out of air, having been underwater when the device began. My blood is staining the water, causing another colored wash, mimicking the black one made by her swirling hair.

I'm screaming now. Crying out. I'm begging them to find someone who works there. It seems like no one is doing anything.

It seems like everyone just feels powerless to do anything.

They all just stand there.

Every part of me wants to jump in and either drown or be cut in two to do SOMETHING, ANYTHING to stop this. I can't be watching her die right in front of me.

Can I?

This isn't how people die. This isn't how it happens, I think, as I watch her start to twitch and seize. She's drowning now, her lungs filled with water. She chokes and squirms and moves involuntarily.

Someone else is there, too. Someone else is trying to stop it. Is it Kalista? The sun is in my eyes and I can't see. I can't hear anything but my own screams.

She's yelling, too. The woman in the pool stops moving. In my head, a number counts down. I think about how cool the water is and how much time she could be like that and still be revived. I try to believe.

Some man starts to shoot as the covering closes completely. His second shot bounces off and hits the other woman. Her arm goes limp. Blood splatters out all over the top of the pool covering. I am hammering at it now, trying to break this unbreakable thing, looking for something to use to hammer into this bulletproof glass.

I crawl over to the woman. It is Kalista. I grab her arm and start to wrap my shirt around it. She is crying, hammering at the clear ground below her. I pull her to the side and Finish wrapping up her wound while the manager arrives, finally, unlocking the pool cover.

It's too late, though.

It's all too late.

"Mom"

I looked up and saw Ersi tugging at me from one side of the medbay. Her shirt was tighter around her and her hair was longer.

She looked to be about six years old.

"Are you ok?"

"Yes, I'm fine. It was a bad dream. I didn't mean to wake you up."

"You didn't. But you were crying. Why were you crying?"

"It was just a dream. A dream about something that happened a long time ago."

"I'm sorry that happened."

She jumped up on the bed next to me and looked at me. She might have been a little older than six. And it was now jarring how much she looked like me. Her skin was that same soft smooth brown that Dae always said she loved so much. She had my nose, for sure, strong and dominant on her face, over my wide mouth and full lips. And her hair was the same mottled dark brown that mine had been since birth, lively and thick and naturally full around her face. Her shape, her laugh.. All of it.

All of it was mine.

"It's ok, Ersi, it's not your fault."

"I just mean I feel bad for you."

"Well, thank you. You weren't sleeping?"

"I don't sleep that much."

"You are talking so well now. You know that?"

"Thank you." and there it was. The six year old girl getting a compliment from her... from her mother?"

"Ersi, do you know where you come from?"

"I come from you, silly. I think that's obvious."

"We sure do look alike, don't we?"

"We do."

"But do you know why you're here? And How?"

"I'm here to help you"

"To help me? To help me do what?"

"To help you. With what you're doing here. To finish the mission."

"So you're here to help me finish the mission?"

"I finish the mission. I told you before."

'What about me?"

"I AM you. Mom. Can't you see that?"

"And what did you mean when you said there wasn't enough space?"

"For everyone. For all of you. All of us. But you said we have to make it work."

"So you're going to help make it work."

"I already told you. Twice I think."

"You told me what twice?"

"Mom. you're forgetting. And that isn't helping."

"I'm sorry. I don't mean to forget. But what did I forget? How can I fix it?"

"Mom. You can't fix it anymore. I have to fix it." She stood up and ran out of the medlab.

"Wait, Ersi, come back." I slipped off the bed and followed her.

She turned left and ran down the starboard corridor that led to the storage area and it was a dead end. I turned after her and ran. She was faster than she should have been. I moved through the corridor and realized that it was longer than it should have been. This should have been the door to the back storage area right next to me. But, instead, it stretched out in front of me.

I saw her shirt for a second in front of me and I dug my heels in and continued to run. The walls to either side of me seemed farther apart now as I seemed to enter a larger area of the halfway, one I was unfamiliar with. I yelled out after her.

"Ersi, stop. Hold on. Stop."

I could hear her breathing now, mixed in with...something else. Some kind of machinery was whirring. The ground below me was becoming more uneven, covered in metal parts, shavings, even pieces that looked mechanical. I slid and fell against the wall, twisting my ankle.

I sat on the floor against the wall and looked out. It was dark and I tried to activate the lights around me. Nothing. I pulled out my own light and it seemed weaker than usual. Pulling myself up against the wall I listened for her voice again. It seemed to be coming from my right.

I pointed my light to the right and saw another corridor branching off form the sternward back corridor. I tried to move as quickly in that direction as I could. I kept calling out but I could barely hear her now.

I looked around me now and I could see that the area was substantially larger than anything I'd seen on the ship so far. It looked cluttered and messy, with pieces of metal everywhere. I tried stepping over the junk so as to not further damage my foot. I pointed my light around, trying to get a sense of where she might have gone.

"Ersi. Come on back. Please. Just let me talk to you."

I was trying to think about what she meant. Did she think we were the same person? Did she think it was her job to replace me? All of this was further confused by the relationship between the two of us. I didn't realize until now how my mind and body were responding to being called someone's mother. It was emotionally manipulative in a way and I wondered if that was the point. Did she mean it or was it to put me off guard.

My conversations with her never seemed to suggest that she was that cunning. But this was a definitive problem.

"Ersi. It's me. Mom. Can you come back?"

I heard a shuffle from up ahead. And a tiny voice.

"Mom. Go back to sleep. Just go to sleep."

I stepped toward the voice.

"Are you okay? Are you over here, Ersi?"

I used her name, hoping it would have some effect on her, some grounding. I realized that parents had been doing this since forever.

"Can you come back?"

I saw her shirt wave up ahead and I started walking faster. What was going on here in this alien part of the ship?

"Please, just go to sleep."

"Why don't you want me to find you. Ersi?" I squinted in the dark , trying to make out what was happening. As I looked forward, it seemed like there were two figures - a smaller one and a larger one. I moved quickly toward them. They were talking. Ersi was talking with a man up ahead. As i got closer I could see. She was facing me but he was facing away. I called out.

"Marin. Is that, you?"

He didn't turn around. They were unmoving, talking. I increased my pace. How had he not heard me.

"Marin. It's me. It's the captain. What's going on?"

Ersi was deep in conversation with him. She was waving her hands and speaking. I strained to hear but I couldn't make out what it was.

"Marin. Stop her. I need to talk to you both."

At that moment I could see his back arch. He stood up straight and then leaned into the wall. He turned his head outward and back toward me. And I saw it.

Where his face should have been was a smooth expanse of skin.

Just as we'd seen on the video with Lyra. I called out. He turned back to Ersi and seemed to fold up, like a piece of paper, jerking left then right, then folding top to bottom. I screamed out, "Marin!" and he folded again and again.

Until he was sucked into what looked like a hole in the wall to his left.

Ersi looked up and stared at me. She shook her head and ran. I took a breath and pushed myself, trying to catch up but my light started to fade. The lights all around me went dead and a tiny corona of visibility shrunk like a melting ball of wax leaving me dead in the dark. I turned and hit my head.

And then I felt myself fall.

-8 Days

I had to find someone within forty eight hours. After that, there isn't any hope. Everything degrades so fast in this world, I remember thinking. It doesn't matter how beautiful and immense and amazing it is.

It's still gone in forty eight hours.

I met him at a crowded bar. At that time, everything in the world was crowded. There was no way to meet, to talk, to ask for help, to bribe, to cajole, anything in private. Earth was full. Full of everyone but the person who should have been there.

I'm sure I wasn't the only person to think that.

We went into a room behind the bar and spent precious moments talking. It was small and white and sterile looking.

"Can I see that again?"

"My id?"

"I never saw a captain's ID before."

I pulled it out again and placed it on the table between us.

"And you're not... you know?"

I shook my head.

He moved his tongue around in his mouth as though he was just finishing off a big meal. Thinking, trying to consider if he should trust me.

"I should check."

I stood up and put my arms out. He gingerly stepped up to me and put his hands on my waist. He pressed the backs of his hands against my chest, my waist, my legs.

I was clean.

"Is that it?" He nodded his head at the small temp drive sitting next to where I'd put my ID.

"We don't really have a lot of time."

He looked at me. He could tell I was a mess. So much so that it must have dug at him and pulled out a nurturing tone.

"We're good for a while. You got here on time."

"So how do we do this?" I wrapped my hoodie around my shoulders. I was suddenly cold.

"It's easy. Hell, you should know, right?"

"That's right."

"With what you do…"

"I understand."

People come here because they don't want anyone to know. Because I'm discreet, right?"

"Yes."

He looked me up and down and, it seemed, finally decided i wasn't a threat.

"You're going to hurt for a bit after."

I wanted to grab him by the shoulders and scream into his face and tell him that it hurt NOW. It hurt impossibly right now. But I sat there and tried to let the numbness wash over me.

"How do you want to start."

He tossed me a gown and pulled a small white bottle from the refrigerator in front of him. "Put this on." Placing the bottle on the table. "And drink this."

I stood up and looked at him. For a moment it looked like he wanted me to undress in front of him. Until I realized. I pulled out my phone and showed it to him. I clicked and his phone buzzed like a tiny cash register.

"That's it." he said. He turned around and I pulled the gown un, removing my clothes under it. I didn't understand why I needed to be undressed but I'm told it has something to do with the electronic connections.

I took a deep breath and drained the bottle completely.

I woke up in the present to Dae shaking me in the medlab.

"Zoo, are you ok? Fuck."

"What the... Dae, where is Marin?"

"We can't find him. It's like Lyra. Not on the ship."

"Damn, where is Ersi?"

"She's in the Den."

"Hold her. I'm coming."

I dragged myself off the Medbay bed. I could feel the pressure on my ankle I'd twisted last night. I limped down the starboard corridor to the Den.

Ersi was sitting at the table with the three remaining crewmembers. I grabbed her arm.

"What the hell?"

She looked up at me terrified. She looked to be about seven years old now. I could see she'd been crying.

Ro started, "Marin is gone."

"I know. I ran after her last night and she was with him when he disappeared."

"The video shows both you and her in bed all night."

"Bullshit."

Kal came over to my side of the table, "It really does, Zed."

"Show me."

Ro flicked the video onto the main monitor. It was at 3x speed. I saw myself climb into bed with Ersi still asleep. Not long after, Marin woke up and walked out, as if in a trance.

He didn't return.

"Is that it?"

"That's all. You and this one slept all night. You looked like you were having some pretty bad dreams."

I looked at the version of me on the monitor. I remembered the pool dream and wondered if what I had seen was an extension of that.

"Do you remember talking to me last night, late?"

Ersi looked at Ro and then back at me. She shook her head., "I don't. Mom, I slept all night."

"And it looks like so did you."

"My ankle is twisted. It hurts."

Ro fast forwarded the video. "Watch." At one point, my foot shot out and hit the side of the bed. You could almost feel the impact. I was sleeping.

"What the fuck."

Dae reached over to me, "what were you dreaming?"

"It started with… It doesn't matter. You can't find Marin?"

Kalista handed me the pad. No sign of him anywhere.

"I don't believe I dreamed that last night."

"I don't know how he got off the ship." Dae looked confused. "There was nothing, no open airlock notifications, nothing."

"Follow me." I grabbed Dae and made my way to the port corridor by the medbay. Ro followed us.

"Zed, what are you doing?"

"Just follow. Come here."

"This goes in a circle."

And it did. The corridor was back to normal. It snaked around the back of the engine room and returned, in a circle.

Back to where it started.

But last night, I ran almost a kilometer down this corridor. And then watched Marin disappear. He was standing with the clone. She said something to him.

Ro examined the passage. It was normal. It was exactly as it was on the specs.

"There's no exit from the ship this way."

"We need to look for a doorway, anything."

"I don't see anything. Not even a break in the wall. Nothing."

"Was Marin acting strange yesterday at all?"

Ro looked at me, "He was normal. He was happy, if anything. I thought he was weathering the weirdness here more than we were."

"Why did you think that?"

"I don't know. I saw him laughing with Ersi at one point. He seemed to be enjoying taking care of her."

"That's what I thought, too."

"If he left this ship. He and Lyra both, they are gone. They are atomized."

"What if he's still here somewhere? I mean, we can't just believe anything anymore."

"Got it. Look, Dae, I need you to get back to Kal and the clone. I don't want Ersi alone with anyone anymore. Two people on her at all times. Ro and I are going to look through every inch of the ship."

"Aye, Captain. Be careful." She gave me a kiss and returned back down the corridor.

"Did you chart this area again on the pad?"

"I did yesterday. It was the same. No growth."

"Let's make the round here and look through the storage areas and workshop areas, then make our way back to the to the stem."

"Aye, Captain. Starboard Quarter Storage. This is meant to be four meters by four meters square."

"Ok, is there something in front of this door?"

"There wasn't yesterday. Maybe I knocked something over."

Ro pushed the door open, slamming into it with his right shoulder. A metal box had shifted in front of the door, blocking it. I reached in and moved it away, letting it fall to one side. We moved inside the room.

"I'm not getting any readings here. And it looks about right. "

"Hand me the lighttape?" He tossed it to me and I flashed it against the walls in front of me and to my left. This room appeared to be four meters by four meters with a diagonal cut for the hull.

And no sign of Marin.

HE sat down on a box and rubbed his shoulder. He had a large pad on it and it seemed more delicate than it had.

"Let me see that," I pulled off the pad and unwrapped it. "Holy shit."

There was about six centimeters of growth of a small right arm and hand.

"Yeah, it's growing back. Kind of fast. It feels like I may have sprained my tiny arm."

"Maybe. Maybe you even broke it. You have to be all masculine with your left for a bit, i think."

"Yeah. it's... it's certainly. Something."

"Does it hurt?"

He pulled the wrapping back on and slid the pad into place. "Not really, honestly. But ever since this happened, I have this weird feeling."

I pulled up a seat on a box across from him. "What kind of feeling?"

"It's nothing. We have bigger stuff going on."

"No, tell me. I feel like there is a puzzle here and I don't want to be like those shitty movies where it would be over in ten minutes if everyone just told the truth about everything, you know? It's all relevant."

"Ok, I never felt like this before this. But now?"

"Yes?"

"I feel like I don't belong here."

"Hm. have you talked to Dae about that?"

"No, why?"

"That's something that she just said a few days ago. After you found those names on that stowaway storage unit."

"Yeah, I don't think those mean anything. And I never felt that way before this."

"Well, we're going to be planetside in a little over a week. Can you hang in there?"

"Aye, Captain. I'm in."

"Let's check the Keel Deck and get back. I don't see anything here.

Ro got up and moved with me to the back of the Medbay, taking the stemway stairs to the lower deck. He made it down there first with a little splash.

"Shit. Careful coming down here. The floor is covered in about two centimeters of water."

"I fanned the light out. Across the entire lower stem, there was water.

"Is this going to be a problem, you think?"

"I don't think so. I mean, the whole stem is going to take on water when we land. The hydraulics work perfectly well underwater."

"What about the underside of the engine room?"

"It's sealed from down here. And forward stowage isn't even accessible here. So…"

"Should we be worried about where it came from?"

"Yeah, I'm trying to run that through my brain right now. There is so little here it might actually be condensation from a temperature differential."

"But no Marin?"

"No where. Sensors say what we see. He's not on board, dead, alive, anything. Gone."

"And no activity from the air locks, either side?"

"Nope."

"Is there another one of those doors here?"

Ro flashed his light against the walls. The lower deck was as wide as the main one but less long. The stem was about the size of half of the Den plus the medlab.. It was still substantial. We moved along the port side.

"Do you see that? There."

Ro pointed to the corner. Right where the port wall met the fore curve. There it was.

Another door.

The people who had signed up to fly on the Leviathan all had one thing in common. In one way, they shared the sentiment that Ro had expressed.

They no longer felt like they belonged on Earth.

And that feeling made them desperate enough to get onto a sleeper ship aimed at earth's closest possibly inhabited neighbor and sleep as the ship slowly made its way to its new home.

They put their hopes in the fact that, at some point in the twenty years before they arrived, There would be innovations that would make it possible for cargo to meet them. There would be food, lodging, doctors, all of it, waiting.

Assuming that human advancement and innovation followed its steady and reasonable path to progress.

In many ways this group of over seventeen thousand people had more faith than even the most ardent religious adherents in history. Their religion? A seamless and perfect faith in the continuing story of man's scientific evolution.

And their church was a ship that drew inexorably closer to the same planet we were closing in on now.

For our part, we had to mirror that faith. We had to believe in the newer, more experimental technology that allowed the EckoShips to work.

When we landed, it would be in a state of twilight. It would be up to the ship to take care of the few steps needed before we could work on this planet and make it ap;ropriate for the job of colonization.

So it was incredibly important that this ship function as it was supposed to.

We returned to the Den and found Dae, Kal, and Ersi sitting in the Galley. Ersi was looking at me strangely, her head down. She looked to have aged nearly a bit even as we were exploring. She looked so much like a smaller version of me it was hard to focus. I went over to her side of the table.

"Hey. I'm sorry I freaked out at you. Marin is missing and I could have sworn I saw you with him. I know the cameras show something different and it's not your fault. But this is really freaking us out. Do you remember anything at all from last night?"

She looked as though she were almost about to cry. I wanted to reach out and find a way to make her time on this ship less chaotic. I don't know where she came from, but there was no reason she had to be miserable.

"Can I ask you a question?"

She wiped a tear away, "Sure."

"You don't remember being up at all last night?"

"No, I slept all night."

"Do you remember telling me before that there wasn't enough space?"

"Did I say that?"

"You did, sweetheart." her eyes darted over to Kal, who nodded.

"Do you remember why you said that?"

"It just seemed like there wasn't enough room."

Kal leaned in, "For what, sweety? What isn't there enough room for?"

"For this." She waved at us. "For all of you."

I looked at everyone.

There were four of us now, from the original crew and he had less than eight days left to go.

We searched the top deck for anomalies, too, and found nothing. We ate mostly in silence as we all tried to figure out, in our heads, what was happening. Kal had found an education database in the ship files and set Ersi up in front of a monitor. We really had no idea how she was developing like this but the resources on the planet would help us figure it out. We'd be down a medical officer and a bio officer, but there should be enough information int eh databases to hopefully make up for it. I tried not to let myself agonize over Lyra and Marin until we could once and for all figure out what had happened. They both seemed to have willingly left the ship while it was under warp, knowing full well it would kill them.

I took a bite and turned my head to Ro. He was deep in thought.

"Hey, guys. This is crazy."

I was willing to entertain crazy.

"Does it mean anything that Lyra was the one person on the crew none of us really knew? And then Marin was the one we knew second least?"

"What do you think it could mean?"

"I don't know. I'm just thinking. Looking through the dynamics of the crew."

"Okay. So how would that work?" Kal tried to see it.

"So you and Kal, you've been friends since Grade school, basically. You and Dae are really close, obviously. You, me and Kal have been on missions together over and over again. The four of us are really, pretty close."

"Right?"

"We knew Marin from around the base. And until this mission, none of us knew Lyra at all."

"Is that true? I remember her giving me my physical before I left for this mission. But she said she didn't remember it."

Dae leaned in, "Don't you think that's weird?"

"Yes, but I have no idea what it means. Do any of you remember getting your physical before you came?"

Ro looked up "I mean I've had literally a thousand physicals."

"Do you think it means something that we knew them less?"

"Maybe it was something that made them feel like they didn't belong here. Like subconsciously?"

"When you pushed that door open. When you lost your arm, is that how it felt to you?"

He sat back and looked to his right at Ersi. She was sitting cross legged in the lounge, fascinated by a monitor.

"I don't... It's kind of hazy. It was like a weird compulsion. I didn't have the sense I didn't belong. I just had this feeling like it was time to go."

"Time to go?"

"Yeah, like it was my time to get out of here. At that moment. Like it was time."

"And that feeling went away."

"It did, it kind of..." Ro took a deep breath. "I felt like it was time to just get out. And the feeling, it sort of lingers. It hangs on me. Like I have to go."

"Do you know where you are supposed to go?" Dae whispered?"

"No. just not be here anymore."

I looked through my head to see if I had felt that at any time. I hadn't. Why was I so sure i belonged here and should be here when other people here were not so sure at all.

What was different about me?

-7 Days

In the 1960s, NASA had built out a large testing facility in Hancock County, Mississippi that would allow it to test larger rockets and space-forward structures. Over the next one hundred and ninety years or so it had grown bigger and bigger until, by the 2130's it was the largest single business institutional space in the world.

It was called Stennis Space Center. And in 2130, I was fourteen years old, starting my very first internship there, full of random space knowledge and wanting nothing more than to contribute somehow to the purposeful drive to discover through space exploration. Within a year, I was put on command track. I was told that they were good at identifying leadership when they saw it.

And that was me, apparently.

The truth is that I was used to being the oldest one around in a house full of younger kids, cousins, etc. Even the neighbor kids I babysat. My mother had me when she was young, before she started sorting out her life, so sometimes I even kind of parented her. Was I ready to lead people? I guess so.

I was excited but that meant a different path than I had anticipated. I figured I would be an engineer, that I would work in hard science, technology, physics. And there certainly was a lot of that.

But as an XO, commander, or captain, I would have to be well versed on everything that happened on the ship, from the psychology of the crew to biology, medical, hardware, software, life support, navigation, all of it. I would have to be a self contented system that could make sense of everything that needed to be done, and allocate work when needed.

I needed to change my own personal idea of who I was.

In school, I was focused, directed, and I never had much use for people who claimed to be a jack of all trades. But out here, that's exactly what I had to be because no matter the discipline, I had to be the final decision maker.

And that meant being sort of the king of the jack of all trades.

We had all slept in the lounge that night. I was understandably reluctant to let anyone out of my site at all after the last few days. I kept Ersi near me. Because, as much as I had thought about Ro's breakdown of the ship dynamics, a slightly different idea had been gnawing at me.

Lyra had spent the most time with Ersi and she was the first to go. After that, Marin had found a way off the ship. And I couldn't help but notice he had spent the second most amount of time with her.

If Lyra or Marin were here I would have brainstormed with them the idea rolling around in my head. Could this be a virus with neurological implications? - a virus that made people feel as though they needed to escape, get out, be away?

Without Marin or Lyra, I was the one on the ship with the most understanding of biology and that was mostly restricted to a biochemistry bachelors in college and everything I could pick up on the job. Which, truth be told, was a lot. .

I realized sitting across from her at breakfast, this miniature version of me that looked all of eight years old, precious, endearingly calling me "mom," acting now more than anything like a part of the crew, that I was not the right captain for this situation. I had always had a soft spot for kids and, as someone who had grown up in that big family, with kids all over, it was hard for me to turn a skeptical eye toward this clone who looked so much like just another member of my family.

Was I being targeted somehow?

Was this a tactic designed to work on me?

Was this sweet little girl some kind of an attack or just an accident of cell growth in an experimental ship on a trip that seemed to be delivering more questions than answers?

"Ro, I'm hoping you and Dae can stick closely together and help map out any additional changes in this ship. Kal, you and I are going to take Ersi to the medlab and run some epidemiology studies."

Ro grabbed a pad and started planning. "Got it." Between him and Dae, there wasn't an inch of this ship they didn't understand. I didn't know what to expect, but my hope was they could watch out for each other. I wasn't looking to lose anyone else.

We made our way out the galley door down the Starboard Corridor. Which led to our first discovery of the day.

The door to Pod five was missing. This meant that Marin's pod was gone, just like Lyra's had disappeared.

I looked at Kal and she felt the smooth wall right across from the starboard lounge door. It looked as though it had been constructed from one solid piece of metal. There was no sign a door had ever been there.

"Ersi, Do you see this?"

"Yes, mom."

"There was a door here. There was a room here before."

She looked at me and cocked her head a bit.

"Can you imagine where it might have gone?"

She felt the wall. "Do you think it just wasn't needed anymore?"

Kal tried this time, "Does that make sense to you? That rooms would disappear if they aren't needed?"

She shrugged. I wondered if she had enough experience in the world to realize how truly strange this was or if it all just seemed normal to her. I tried to remind myself that even though she looked like an eight or nine year old girl and talked almost like an adult that she was still only about a week old. I didn't know what that might mean for her ideas around object permanence and the persistence of forms.

I kneeled down, "Ersi, how does it make you FEEL that the ship is changing so much?"

"It's ok, Mom, it probably needs the room somewhere else."

"Is that what's supposed to happen?"

Ersi stared at me for a second and then slowly nodded her head. She took my hand and led us to the Medlab.

The space at the back of the Medlab was still extended a bit. That should have created a bulge in the transom way behind this space but it didn't, just like the bulge in the area in the back of the den didn't seem to impact the integrity of the medlab. Thinking too hard about that was terrifying so I tried to compartmentalize. One mystery at a time.

Kal set up the tray for me while I knelt down to talk to Ersi.

"Can I lift you up and put you on the bed here?"

"What's going to happen to me?"

"Nothing, sweetheart. We just need to run some tests."

"What kind of tests?" She crossed her arms and I was afraid this might be the start of some poorly timed defiance. I toyed with the idea of not being fully straight with her, but decided that this might be a good teachable moment.

"Well, let me ask you, do you know the difference between the truth and a lie?"

Her browns dipped as she looked at me. "The truth is when you say what is really happening and a lie is when you don't."

"Very good. Now, I want to say the truth to you, always. You and I should be truthful with each other."

"Are you going to kill me?"

I stood up. That was unexpected. "My God, why would you ask me that?"

Kal looked up over the test equipment curiously. How had Ersi even come up with this concept?

"When I was tiny, you wanted to throw me off the ship." she made a motion with her fingers, representing how tiny. Very tiny.

Kali stepped over, "Who told you that, sweetheart?"

"I heard it. Mommy said it."

"That's not- " I looked at Kalista, "That's not possible.You were just a bunch of cells, sweety. I didn't realize…"

Kal tousled her hair, " Sweetheart, you couldn't have heard that yourself, though, right? You didn't even have ears."

"I told you I know what the truth is and what a lie is."

"That's not possible. But Ersi, no one wants to hurt you."

"You promise?"

Kal stood up straight and crossed her heart, "We promise."

She held her hands up so that I could lift her onto the medbay bed. I picked her up. She was surprisingly heavy, a grim reminder of how accelerated her unexplained growth was. I tried to keep her occupied while Kal took a cell sample. I looked down at her hands and pulled a slip of blue carbon backed paper out of the drawer next to the bed. Kal looked over.

"What are you doing?"

"Just trying to set my mind at ease."

"You know that's not possible, either."

"Kal, what part of this is possible?"

"What would it even mean if your fingerprints match?"

"I don't know. The odds are absurdly against it. I get it"

"Not just absurdly. Like there aren't enough atoms in the ship. And, ok, I don't see anything epidemiological here. No viruses, nothing. And her DNA. I mean, it's just you."

"I'm just like you, mommy. See?" Ersi held up her finger, blue now from the carbon sheet. I nodded as Kal looked at me. I held up my finger, too. It was also blue.

"That isn't... There isn't."

"I know. Fingerprints are made in the womb, they aren't part of a DNA phenotype. But we have the same fingerprints."

Kal put the sample dish down and backed off.

"Ok, let's try and think about this for a minute. You have a clone that is growing exceptional fast without an accelerator, has access to language and information from before she had a brain, without an overlay, and shares your post natal features."

"That's it in a nutshell."

"Is that unusual? Am I doing something wrong?" It was too easy to forget that Ersi was listening in, hearing everything." I put my hand over hers.

"No, sweetheart. You aren't doing anything wrong. We're just confused."

"What are you confused by?"

"Well…" I thought I would continue down the road to absolute candor. "We're confused about you. Do you know why you are growing so fast?"

"Oh. It's so I can do my job when we get to the planet."

Kalita jumped in, "Do you know what that job is?"

"Of course, silly. We have to make Proxima B into something good for the people coming."

Kal and I looked at each other. I don't know if Marin had used the name of the planet, but I had never and I could see from the look on Kal's face that she hadn't, either. So how did she know the name of the planet? I took a deep breath.

"But that's my job, baby. I'm supposed to do that job."

"I'm not a baby. And I already told you over and over, I can take over the job. It's my job now."

"I don't remember you saying that, Ersi."

"You keep forgetting important things, Mommy."

"Do I?" I sat on the bed next to her and tried to look unimposing. "What am I forgetting?"

She looked uneasily at Kal

"Kal, do you have anything else to check?"

She took a breath. "I have one more sample I was going to look at. I'll leave you two." She stepped over to the table in the center of the room. I leaned in and whispered to Ersi.

"What am I forgetting, sweety?"

"Everything, Mommy. We talked about this. You can relax. I can take over for you. You can let go?"

"Let go? What do you mean, let go?"

"You can just let go. You know. You don't have to carry it all anymore. That's why I'm here."

"What am I carrying?

"Dae, Kal, Ro, everyone. You can let them go."

"Do you mean let them leave the ship?"

Kal called out, "Zedi, you need to see this."

I ignored her, placing my hand on Ersi's arm, "Do you want them to leave the ship?"

"This is important, Zoo,"

"What is it Kal?"

"I brought a sample of the undifferentiated cells from Ro's arm on a whim. I just tested them."

"They're his cells, right? Stem cells?"

"They're stem cells, but they aren't his. They're yours."

"What. That's nuts." I backed away from Ersi. It hit me hard.

"They're yours, aren't they?"

"It's ok, mommy."

"I leaned over and fell against the table, sending a metal tray clattering to the ground. Ersi could see the look in my eyes- Mine and Kal's both.

We were afraid.

She jumped down off the table and ran toward the back of the room. I called out without thinking, "Grab her."

I could see her curve right toward the transom way and I ran out, watching her run across the back, behind the lab. Kal was right by my side as we chased her across the transom way to the other side of the ship. She turned right again.

"Ersi. Come back." She ran across the Transom way with the security of someone who was born on the ship, which, I remembered, she was. We called after her as we ran.

Kal and I doubled back to the Medlab. I saw Ersi's mop of hair, so similar to mine, descend the stemway stairs. When we reached the bottom there was a larger splash than I had anticipated. Flipping on my light I could see that the entire floor of the stem was still underwater, and the water level had risen. It was nearly four centimeters all throughout the room now.

Kal had pulled out her light, too. "Holy fuck, Zed, this room is huge now."

"Ersi? Can you hear me. This is mom…"

I called for the lights to flick on to no effect. Something was wrong with the lighting. I took another step and asked Kal. "Can you feel that? The floor? It feels uneven. It doesn't feel the same."

"Yeah, it's almost an organic feeling."

"Do you see her?"

Kal shook her head and shined her light on her face. "Zed. I think I know that's happening."

"Great, spill it, because I got nothing."

"Because it's not your job. It's mine. When we land, part of my job is to set up the terraforming tools in the aft cargo hold. They will start to transform the planet for the Leviathan people to live on."

"Ok, right."

"Do you see? This? All of it?"

"I don't get it."

"These machines got triggered somehow."

"That doesn't sound very scientific."

"Ok, let that go, somehow they were turned on. They are trying to terraform the ship."

"That's insane. How would that even…"

"I know it is, but it fits."

I lifted my light forward. "Ersi!"

I listened for footsteps int he water, but it was quiet. I could hear Kal breathing next to me.

"What's that?" Kal pointed to an area about ten meters away. I could see there was a white spot on the wall. The water splashed under us with every step as we stepped forward, lights trained on the wall.

I recognized it right away. I turned to Kal to see if she did, too.

A number six enclosed in a circle.

There was still no sign of Ersi when we got to the Den. But something she said was still gnawing at me. None of the ship's sensors could locate her, but, again, one mystery at a time.

"Can you show me the video for the last call we got before the drive was initiated?" I was done pretending I had all the information I needed to make decisions. It was time to do some deep diving.

Ro pulled out a pad, "I should be able to." He started rifling through the archives.

"What's wrong?"

"Nothing. I know it's here."

"Can you tell me anything about the call? Any information?"

"I'm not sure…" He was still looking.

"Ro, you were there. You were on that call"

"I honestly can't remember."

"You told me you were. I skipped it and you said you were on it."

"I can't find the actual recording."

"Can you find the room recording from the call?" I was starting to wonder if he was there. Had he lied to me? Why would he?

That was nuts.

"I think so. Ok. I can show the signoff. I have a small clip."

"Where is the rest?"

"I'm still looking but it doesn't look like it's here."

"What do you have?"

"One sec." he flicked the short video onto the main monitor. It showed me, alone, standing in front of a screen.

"That's not it. I wasn't there. I was with Dae."

Dae nodded and reached for my hand

"This is it." The camera was adjusting and moving around me. But it was me. I could see my face.

"Do you have any audio?"

"I'm trying to find it. I don't know why it's not here."

It was the strangest thing looking at myself smiling and responding to the screen, when I knew, for a fact I wasn't there. I had missed this call. This couldn't be me. Was it another clone somehow?

"Nothing? Audio""

"Nothing. I'm sorry."

We all looked up at the screen. Kal saw it first.

"Fuck. Look."

The camera panned around me and darkened as it caught the light from the screen head one. There was a flash then, over my shoulder, we could see who was on the screen.

It was Lyra.

Da dropped my hand. "That's not right."

I looked at Ro, "This is doctored. Who did that?"

Ro raised his arms, "I didn't touch it. I don't remember any of this."

I stared upward. There was no doubt about it. On the call, from earth, was Lyra Tambor, the doctor who had come with us. How was that possible?

"Does she have a twin? This is fucked"

Kal looked at me, "No twin, no lookalike. That's her." She leaned into the screen.

"But she was on the ship with us. I know it. We know it, right?"

There were nods around the table as we all tried hard to remember. She was here. The ship's doctor.

Lyra was here.

I looked up at the screen and stepped back a bit, watching myself sign off with someone I was positive was here all along. My head was spinning. I watched my doppleganger turn to leave and a yelled out to Ro, "Stop. Pause it here."

I looked around the room. Terrified of what I couldn't remember. That was me. I was sure of it. Just as I was sure it couldn't have been. He paused it. It hit me hard as I realized.

I felt everything spin around me and I stared. This made no sense.

I pointed to the monitor.

"What room did this happen in?"

-6 Days

It had been hours since we'd seen Ersi and all we had were unanswered questions. The four of us assembled the rest of our necessary personal items and huddled in the Den. Ro had programmed alarms that would go off if any of us left the area or if Ersi reappeared.

"Dae, can we set the computer to default to audio mode?"

"Sure. Do you want to keep channels open throughout the ship?"

"Yep, I want constant audio alerts as to the shape and configuration of the ship. If anything changes at any time."

"Got it."

Kal pulled a blanket up over her legs and sunk into the couch. "There's literally nothing for us to actually do until we're planetside."

"Except keep this ship from falling apart." Ro looked up from the console where he was helping Dae set up the system.

"Computer"

A slightly flanged but pleasant female voice came from the walls, "Yes, captain."

"Can you locate Ersi anywhere on the ship?"

"I can not find an ERSI with my sensors."

"Alert me when you do?"

"Yes, Captain."

Dae looked up confused. "I don't like the way the computer said that"

Ro tried again, "Computer, do you know who Ersi is?"

"ERSI is an acronym for Extraction and Reintegration System Interface."

Dae shook her head. If any one of us knew, she would.

"Computer, what is that?"

"It is an integrated computer program, Captain."

"What is it integrated with?"

"It is part of the ship's Engram Consciousness Kinesthetic Overlay that enables it to function."

Kal looked confused, "Why would she call herself that?"

"I'm more interested in how she would know. She seems to have this delusion that she needs to finish this mission."

"And replace you."

"It looks that way."

Ro moved to the dock near the galley and opened it, pulling out a gun. "So you are in danger."

"Hold on. We need to be careful, obviously, shooting anything in here. I can't have any holes in this ship."

"I'll set this to a low caliber. It's basically a controllable brad nailer. It won't pierce metal. It will pierce people."

"I also don't want to kill a little girl, no matter how mistaken she is."

"She knows things she shouldn't know. And, hell, who knows how big she even is now. These cells growing back my arm. She's controlling them?"

"I don't know. I don't know why you would have my cells on you. Or hers. Or whatever." Ro held out his right arm, very nearly as long as his left now. And outside of the fact that the color was darker, close to my own, it looked like his arm.

But it wasn't. Not really.

He lifted the gun.

"Ro, put that down. Now."

"I'm sorry, Captain. I think you're in danger."

"Mr. Acosta, do not point a gun in my ship."

"She's going to hurt you. She wants to take your place."

Kal stepped toward him. "C'mon, buddy. Give me that."

He swiveled and pointed it toward her. I stepped forward, "Mr. Acosta, drop that gun right now. Ro."

"Captain. I can't put it down."

"Give it to me."

I reached for the gun, lunching, only to see it disappear before I could grab it. "What the fuck."

Kal and Dae stared. Did a gun just disappear into nothing right in front of us?

"Ro, what is happening?"

"I don't know, Captain. This arm."

"Can you control the arm?"

"Fuck that," Dae looked terrified, "How did it make a gun disappear. I saw it."

"We all saw it." Kal was just as scared.

"It hurts, Captain. Zed, it hurts."

"Stand down, Ro. Let me help."

Ro held up his arm. It seemed to shimmer - to move beneath the surface. "I don't know what's happening."

I reached out and grabbed him. He was burning up.

"Captain, it's so hot. It's hot in here."

I tried to calm him down, holding his arms down. "Computer, what is the temperature in the Den?"

"Captain, it's seventy degrees."

"It's hot. I said it's too hot."

Kal looked confused, "Zed, we didn't find any viruses or pathogens but he seems to be sick."

"Yeeah, he's on fire."

"I have to protect you."

"Ro, you have to sit down. You aren't well. We can figure this out."

Dae called out, "what happened to the Galley table?"

It was gone. That was Ro's last project. He spun around and started moving toward where the table was.

"Oh my god. Everything I did. It's all disappearing."

"That's crazy. That's not possible"

"It's me. I'm the next one to disappear. I don't belong here anymore."

I reached out to grab him, "No one is disappearing, Roja."

"Don't LIE TO ME." Ro lifted his right arm and a hundred black tendrils shot out of it, trapping us like insects in a web. They spread across the entire den and moved slowly, seemingly as webbing in a breeze.

"Mr. Acosta, STAND DOWN. Stop it!"

"How is he doing this?" I had Kal in my line of sight. But where was Dae?

"It hurts. It's so hot." He shifted, pressing us against the port wall of the Den. I saw Dae and I started climbing through the tendrils to reach her and Kal.

They were slick and oily, like coherent octopus ink in water, spreading out and filling the room. Ro had dropped to his knees. Whatever this was, it looked like it was killing him.

"Computer, what are these black tendrils?"

"Captain, I do not see any black tendrils."

"Bullshit. What the fuck. Computer identify the substance coming from Mr. Acosta's Arm."

"Captain, I cannot find Mr. Acosta."

"Ahh. See? Stop this, Captain, please. I don't want to go."

"You aren't going, Ro."

His head fell into his left hand. The tendrils shook and hipped around the room, pinning us. They moved toward the inner Den wall almost as though falling, spilling onto the wall in a great black disk.

"I can't be here anymore. I have to go."

"You don't have to go anywhere." I looked over to Kal, "What are these made of?"

"I don't know."

"Computer, break down the composition of space in the Den."

"Captain, I have three life signs, standard furniture and gear and 84.7% breathable air."

"Is that all, computer?"

"Captain!"

Kal was trying to pull a black puddle of tendril from Dae's face. It looked stuck. She couldn't breathe.

"Roja, what are you doing? You need to stop this."

I heard him grunt and then scream. He lifted his head from his left hand and I could see why the scream was so muffled.

His face was gone. In its place was a smooth pale area, eyeless, without a mouth. He tumbled forward as though falling and slammed into me. I reached out to grab the couch and he fell against the Aft Den wall. The black of the tendrils swirled in a circle on the wall like the surface of a well, liquid and smooth. Ro sank into it.

"Kal, is Dae ok," I asked without looking.

"She can breathe. I think she can breathe."

"Roja, hang in there." I swam through the tendrils with one hand, gripping the tops of the furniture with the other. I felt gravity shifting, placing the black disk under me. My legs dropped out from under me as I reached for him.

"Grab my hand."

Ro screamed, muffled, as he fought to stay. His feet pressed against the black disk and he began to sink.

"No. No no. C'mon, buddy. Grab my hand."

The den was full of the sound of his thick muted shrieks against the torrent of the black ooze, looking as though it was eating through the wall of the ship. It sucked him in and I couldn't stop it. Bit by bit, he disappeared into the wall.

Suddenly the lights flashed and the gravity returned to normal, dropping me, Dae, and Kal hard onto the ground. I looked up. The black tendrils were gone and so was Ro. A charred black space remained against the wall. I ran to it and felt it. It was cold and dirty, covered in a kind of black soot. I pushed against it and hammered my fists. It was solid. There were no signs of an opening.

"Zoo" I turned around when Kal called.

She was holding Dae in her arms on the floor. She wasn't moving.

"I can't wake her up."

We slid her onto the aft bed, as far from the portal that had sucked Ro in as possible. The far wall looked the same as always. There was no way to tell that on the other side of it, we'd just seen a man sucked into it.

So where did Ro go?

"Computer, locate Mr. Roja Acosta."

"He is not aboard the ship, Captain."

Dae was breathing and looked as though she may have just been knocked unconscious when one of the tendrils hit the wall.

Kal looked frustrated, "Computer, are your sensors functioning correctly?"

There was a delay of a couple seconds, a millenia for a computer, before it responded, "All my sensors are functioning optimally. Commander Collins."

"Fuck." Kalista didn't seem to believe it. "Zed, ok, I think she's just knocked out."

"Yeah, that's what it looks like to me."

"Where is Ro?"

"I'm not buying anything this computer says automatically anymore. When Dae gets up, we're searching the ship. We're going to find him and we're going to find the clone."

"And then what?"

"Then, for the next one hundred and twenty five hours or so, we're going to tie everyone to a fucking chair and sit perfectly still until this fucking ship stops in orbit around a planet, that's what we're going to do."

"That seems easier said than done."

"Watch me." I looked up at the monitor. Dae was fine. I pulled out a syringe to inject her with adrenaline. We needed to be up and looking around.

"Computer, there is a clone of me on this ship. I need you to find her."

"Yes, Captain. Looking."

"Wait, what are you doing?"

Kal grabbed my arm and slowly removed the syringe from my hand.

"I'm giving her an adrenaline shot to get her back on her feet.

Kal pointed to the bottle on the cart. It read "Fentanyl." I let go of the syringe.

"Holy fuck."

"You almost killed her."

"I keyed that in myself. There is no way I could have gotten that wrong."

"It looks like we can't trust anything right now."

Kal was right. Until we could be 100% sure that everything we were seeing was real, we couldn't risk injecting anyone with anything.

"Jesus." I put my head in my hands and stepped away from the bed. On her own, Dae would likely wake up in about an hour. I needed us to stay together.

"Captain, I have identified the clone's location"

Kal looked at me. "Computer, where is the clone?"

"The clone is directly below you and sixty kilometers to the rear in the engine room."

"Please make that measure again?"

"The clone you are seeking is below you on the keel deck and to the aft sixty kilometers, in the engine room.

I was becoming frustrated as hell, "Computer, this entire ship is only forty meters long on Keel Deck. Do you make that measure?"

There was another endless pause and stoic response.

"Yes, Captain."

"Fuck this. Dae, c'mon." I started shaking her slowly.

"Here." Kal passed a small vial over to me. Smelling salts. Ok. No injection. Much safer. I cracked it and waved it under her nose."

"What - um." she opened her eyes in panic.

"It's ok, D, you're ok. It's safe."

"Where's Ro?" She sat up tentatively.

Kal tried to figure it out while explaining. "He's gone. He disappeared through a kind of portal, made out of that black stuff. The computer can't find him but it says that the clone is on Keel deck, sixty kilometers that way."

"There isn't even six HUNDRED meters that way."

"That's what I said." I searched through the drawers near the beds for something I could use as a weapon - anything.

"The computer's malfunctioning." Dae slid off the bed and tried to test her legs. Kalista helped her stand.

"It doesn't think it is. We know it has to be. Even the med delivery and smaller systems are wonky. We don't really know what's what."

"Well." Dae looked resolute as she pointed. "I know for a fact that sixty kilometers in that direction is fucking outer space.

I handed her a knife from the drawer as I slid my own into my waistband, "Well, try to maintain that certainty."

There was about a meter of water now at the bottom of the stem stairway. It was as dark as I remembered but the bottom was, if anything, even more organic and soft. We could feel the give with every step, almost as if the bottom was sand.

"Computer, Turn on all lights on the keel deck."

"All available lights on keel deck are illuminated, Captain"

"Well, that sucks." Dae pulled out her light and turned it on. The stem area on the keel deck should have been about the same size as the Medbay. But the dark seemed to stretch out for at least fifty meters ahead of us.

Kal squinted and tried to see where it ended. "Ok, so that should be hydraulics, right?"

Dae pointed ahead. "Yes, about ten meters ahead of us at the most is the hydraulics bay. Behind us, here, about fifteen meters is the back wall of the stem area that meets the lower transom way.

About twenty meters starboard should be the lower corridor leading to the landing struts and right here should be the doorway to the port corridor leading to the landing struts on this side. I don't know what any of this is, but it's not this ship."

"Computer, how large is this room?" I called out.

"The room is one hundred meters wide. It ends two hundred meters in front of you. It is unbound in the aft direction, captain, so I am unable to give you an accurate measurement."

"No fucking way." Dae was fully awake now. She pointed the light behind us.

Kal started walking toward the back. "Does unbound mean what I think it means?"

"I think it means there is no aft hull to the ship anymore so let's be careful moving in that direction." I took a quick step so I would outpace her. Sometimes outranking someone means being at least a few centimeters in front of them when crazy unknown shit is happening.

"Zoo, what were you like at twelve years old?"

"Uh. I was fully grown, pretty much." I understood where Dae was headed with this. By this time, the clone would be about twelve. She'd be nearly grown up.

"I was an emotional wreck. I was basically raising my brothers and sisters. You couldn't tell me anything."

"I think that's what we might be stepping into."

Kal stopped. "Before we go any further, we should be on the same page. How are we handling this clone?"

Dae raised her light to illuminate her face, "This thing with Ro, she did that, right?"

"I don't know. The cells on him. They were hers and mine. I didn't do it. I don't understand any of it."

"So she could be as fucked up and in the dark as we are?"

I had considered that. What if she wasn't doing anything? If this wasn't her, she would be just a scared little girl.

"so, this is Fantasia. Is she Mickey Mouse or just some random ostrich?"

Kal looked at me. " I hate the fact that i know what she's talking about"

"Yep. me, too. it's a good point, though."

"Here's the good news. The computer is malfunctioning."

"That is great news."

"I mean it," I continued. "So when it tells us that our people aren't on the ship anymore, I no longer trust it."

"You're right. Everyone could be here, on the ship."

We moved steadily forward. The wall behind us was farther than it should have been, but it was there. We felt our way to the door to the transom way. And walked out. We'd all been here before. But it didn't look like this.

"Ok," Dae started, "this area is really only meant to be a meter and a half wide. It's about twice that."

"Or more."

"Or more."

Kal picked up a few of the rocks we were now stepping on. "Where could these have come from."

I took a look. They seemed organic. "Not paving stones. They are smooth, though, like stones at the foot of a beach. Eroded."

"Xenolith." Kal picked one. It was black.

"What is that?" It was about the size of my thumb.

"Obsidian." Kal handed it to me. "A Xenolith is a stone or artifact that has no earthly business being where it is. This is Obsidine. It's an igneous rock made from cooling magma. There is no way to manufacture it on a space ship."

"So it didn't come from here?" I put it in my pocket. I was now at the point where I had no idea what was important.

Dae ran her hands over the far wall. "This is where there should be signs warning us not to enter.

I felt for the door. "The Engine room."

Dae's face became even more serious. "Zoo, I don't love going in this room without knowing anything about what is happening on the other side of this door. The shielding could be compromised. That's a lot of radiation."

"I think that's fair. But I also believe that we should absolutely not split up. And if there is ANY chance that we can find anyone else from this crew and maybe figure out what is going on, we need to try."

Kal took a deep breath. "Let me ask you this, Captain. With a complement of three people, can we complete this mission?"

"We can, but not well. We don't have the intellectual resources to manage half the crises that could arise on that planet. This was the minimum brainpower needed to do this job. If we can find the missing half of this crew, we need to."

Kal nodded, "So we go in."

"And we be ready to bolt in a heartbeat if anything is compromised." I placed my thumb on the handle and opened the door.

We stepped into a space that looked like it had no ceiling. The far walls, if they existed, stretched kilometers away in the distance. It was huge.

But that wasn't the most obvious thing. As far as the eye could see, there were plants, grass, even trees, rising up to the middle of our chests. It was green and opulent. And none of it belonged here.

"So, Kal, " I started. "You had that theory."

-5 Days

"Hold on. One sec." Dae dropped another of the microtrackers she had been putting together from various electronics we had with us. The engine room was now so huge and none of us wanted to get lost on the way back.

Kal looked frustrated. "No nearby human life signs yet." We'd been walking for almost an hour. The flora around us had changed a number of times and we now found ourselves walking across a fairly this grassy field. At this rate, though, we'd be walking for over ten hours to get to where the computer said the clone was.

"Captain, the clone is about five kilometers closer and approaching."

Assuming the computer was correct, that meant that Ersi was walking toward us, as well. And at a pretty brisk pace.

But why?

It was Dae's turn to be optimistic. "You know, this area is huge. There is no reason that we can't anticipate that Lyra, Marin and Ro are here. Somewhere."

"This can't just be an artifact of the drive bubble. Nothing like this happened with any of the Nanoships."

"Well, captain, it wouldn't be the first time in science where simple behaviors of objects differed widely based on the size." Kal wasn't wrong. But this was so far off, I was more interested in her other theory.

"If the terraformers were doing this, what could we expect?"

"It doesn't make much sense, but, ok. Terraformers are essentially very complex and generalized accelerators. They identify the materials we need to survive, determine where they are on the life cycle and advance them through that life cycle until they are at an optimal place for human life."

"That makes sense."

"So, for example, it can identify that you might have a species of charophycean algae. So, it would latch onto that and accelerate not just the life cycle, but the evolutionary cycle and work until you get, like, a fern."

"Or grass."

"Exactly."

"So, is it possible that they latched onto the clone, and that's why she has been growing this way?"

"That isn't really how they work. And they are simple devices, really. I can't see how they could be responsible for our spatial issues or anything."

"Dae, what do YOU think?"

"I don't know, Zoo. If that's the case, how did they get turned on? And what the fuck is that?" She pointed upward. We had all been trying to avoid thinking about it until we could figure all this out, but the more we walked the more apparent it was that this was real, somehow. Above our heads was a wide blue space, seamless, without sign of solidity.

It was a sky. And in the center of it was a sun. It looked as though it had been moving along with us but it seemed to keep moving, even as we stopped. It was clear that here, time was being affected by the same dynamics affecting everything else, as the sun raced toward a setting position, awash in reddish-orange overtones.

Kal saw it, too, "It looks like it's going to be night in the great engine room soon. What do you think this means for our trip timeline, Captain?"

"I do not know. We may have to set up camp for the night. Are we worried about animals?"

"I wish to fuck I could tell you. We're in new territory now."

"Computer?"

"Yes, captain?"

"Can you calibrate for non-human life forms, too, and give us a proximity alert?"

"Yes, Captain. I can. How would you like that alert?" The computer seemed overly cautious. Almost as though it was aware of its own malfunctions in a way.

"You can just tell us."

"Ok, I identify thirty seven thousand, two hundred and twelve life forms in the surrounding sixty meter radius."

"Holy fuck." Dae looked up.

"Computer, can you limit that to lifeforms with a biomass over ten grams?"

"Yes, Captain. By my measure, there are six hundred and seventeen lifeforms in that area that conform to those parameters."

I caught Kal's eye. It was appreciably darker now.

"Oh, that's better."

We were able to get a fire going before it got completely dark. And in the absence of anything resembling a moon, that's all we had. The Computer was no help anymore in managing the environment. There were over six hundred things within a one hour walk from us bigger than a mouse, any one of which could kill us. And half my crew was missing. But Dae was enjoying breaking rules.

"Can you imagine what NASA would say if we told them we were lighting a fire on the ship?"

"I don't look forward to filing this entire report, honestly."

Kal tossed a few sticks into the fire. "How did the clone get so far away?"

According to the computer, Ersi was heading back this way at a brisk march. It looked like she may have almost been running, which didn't fill me with any comforting thoughts. She wasn't stopping for the night. It seemed like she didn't want to be that far away. "Maybe she got caught up in the expansion?"

Which terrified Dae, ever the scientist. "And if that reverses, what happens to us? We're now at least ten kilometers past the outside hull of the ship, in absolute measurements. If this all ends and snaps back somehow, we are floating in space, behind the natural space of the warp bubble. We'd have inertia."

That part was a little comforting to Kal. "So we'd be just a splatter of atomic particles so fast we'd never feel it?"

"Pretty much."

"Ok, guys. We can 'worst case scenario' this all day long, but that's not going to help us find our missing crew, answers, or the clone. Which, by the way, is the order I'm hoping for." That was the truth. If I could find my people and maybe get an answer or two, I'd be happy never seeing that clone ever again.

And then we heard it.

"Wait. Can you guys hear that? Like a whirring?" I grabbed my knife and light and stood up. The light bounced back from multiple locations around the perimeter, where some prickly looking bushes had grown. Something metallic maybe?

"Can you all see anything?"

"Negative, Captain." Kal stepped to my right. We had been trained for this, in a way. We were supposed to maintain an outward facing circle in a hostile environment. Except our circle was meant to be bigger.

"I see them, here." Dae pointed to the bushes behind us. They were surrounding us. They weren't fast but they were advancing. "What the fuck are they?"

I recognized them first, "They look like Radiolarians. Really big ones. They're usually single celled organisms.

"Where did they come from?"

"Water. Any of the sea water samples we have on board. They're basically plankton coated in silica. These look evolved. Big."

The ones closest to Kal moved forward. She called out, "look out."

A large blue Radiolarian charged her. It looked like a meter long organic tank, with spikes coming out from all sides. Its surface was shiny, sparkly even. And as it got closer it shot a spike out, taking a piece of her calf with it.

"Sonofabitch." Kal dove to one side and we converged to cover her. Suddenly, I wished I had that nail gun that Ro was waving around. I wasn't sure if my knife was even going to be able to cut these things.

"Zoo!" Dae must have been thinking the same thing. She tossed me a thick branch in the shape of a baseball bat. This was better. I advanced on the ones coming at Kal.

"Watch out for the spikes. They shoot."

I swung and connected on the one closest to Kal. It was hard to tell where to aim as they were each fairly symmetrical. A rift opened in the top of it and it skittered away. "This isn't even how evolution works."

"Did you see that?" I yelled out.

They seemed to be advancing almost in a straight line. This left them open to being hit from the side and Dae and I took advantage of that. She flanked Kal who was still favoring her left leg. "These things don't like being hit. They're not fighters. And it's clear we aren't food."

"So what are they doing?"

"They may just be territorial."

I looked around. Kal may have a point. They were to our front and left but none behind us or to the right. "We're being herded."

Kal limped to the right. "You know what? I'm ok with that."

"Deal." We started moving right and forward on a diagonal. We could still make progress. And we could avoid them. I kicked the fire to put it out. It got darker.

"So much for rest." We ran to get cover in the tree line. I tried to cover Kal who was getting the worst of it. A spike spun through the dark and hit her in the arm. A spout of blood shot out in front of us.

We dove behind a thick brachiating tree. The radiolarians held back. They seemed tethered to their territory, for which I was grateful as hell. I ripped the bottom of my shirt to wrap it around Kal's arm. The bleeding was slowing down but she looked to be in pain.

"So no fire, I guess."

"Hold still. I have to tighten this."

"Fuck" she kept her arm still, in spite of the pain. Dae kept lookout, but it looked like they were retreating.

"C'mon. I'll help you up."

"What?"

"Kal, if we're going to rest at all, it's probably going to have to be up a bit." I pointed to the branches above us in the tree. She nodded and put her foot in my hand. I lifted and she started climbing.

"Did you see that?"

"I did." I knew exactly what Dae was getting at."What do you think?"

"Well, what I KNOW is that those things weren't targeting us."

That much was clear. For some reason, they were going after Kal.

And I had no idea why.

We took turns on lookout until the sun rose. Time was as warped as space here, with night only lasting a few hours. From our vantage point in the tree we could see some areas to avoid. Further to our left were herds of what looked like giant tardigrades. It was hard to gauge, at this distance, exactly HOW big.

"Computer, I see a structure about fifteen kilometers in front of us, can you verify?" I wasn't sure how much to truth the small makeshift binoculars that came with our uniforms.

"Yes, Captain. I see it."

"Are there large scale bio-signs in that vicinity?"

"No, captain."

"I hope we can believe that." Dae sounded less than trusting.

"How's our girl?"

Dae looked over at Kal, leaning against the trunk on a branch below us.

"She's good. I think. No infection. She's healing. She can walk."

"Good." I had hopes that the structure ahead of us would have some clues as to the location of our crew. I'd been discussing the logistics with the computer for a good part of the night. We were still underway, but if this was the engine room, what happened to the engines?

I had fewer answers and more questions by the minute. I didn't like the direction of that dynamic.

We made our way to the ground and set off in the direction of the structure. It looked like a small temple from a distance. I had no idea what we would find but it did seem like the clone was headed back this way to the same location. If we stepped up our pace we could be there in two and a half hours, which would be right about when she would be.

We found a bush containing some fruits that looked like bananas, only reddish-orange. The computer read them as edible so I took a bite. They tasted like a cross between coconut and angel food cake with a slight raspberry aftertaste. None of this made any sense, but we picked a few to bring with for the walk.

There were creeks every few hundred meters. Kal explain that the terraformers were designed to create a large number of free running water bodies. We had all, by default, it seemed, signed off on the theory that the environmental changes in the ship were due to the terraformers activating but we still had no concrete answers for the other inconsistencies and issues. Why was the ship getting larger in some places while other rooms were disappearing? Where were our people going and why? And I'd seen the artifact of the missing faces a number of times. I know it wasn't a hallucination.

So what was it?

We climbed a tree or two regularly as we approached. The dimensions around us seemed to be steady and we were closing in on the temple structure. We saw no sign of the clone, though, and that was starting to worry me.

There were unfamiliar smaller animals and insects, none of which seemed to be interested in us at all. That seemed curious to me. Why would the insects be avoiding us? It was almost like we weren't in their food chain - not a part of their environmental integration? Were we missing something they needed to survive? I tossed that idea aside. I should have been grateful. The last thing we needed is to be pursued relentlessly by a cloud of killer insects.

"So what do we do when we see the clone?" Dae asked, revisiting our earlier conversation.

"I say we just hold on to her. Honestly, we have no idea what's going on and best case scenario, she's in as much danger as we are. She has to understand that."

"Kids understand nothing."

"That might be true, but that's my call. For her own good, we have to detain her. No more running around while we don't know what she or the ship is doing. What I want to know, myself, is how there could be what looks like a man-made structure in the middle of all this."

Kal shook her head, "I seriously have no idea. That's not how this works. Terraformers only help build the environment. People have to make the stuff in it. It's not going to just create buildings. That's insane."

"How much evolution do you think it takes to grow a Tardigrade to be three meters tall?"

"That is not... hm. I don't know"

"Why don't you ask her the question you want to ask?" I turned to Kal and saw Ersi, taller and bigger than I'd last seen her, with her arm coiled around Kalista's neck, a knife in one hand. Dae jumped forward but I held her back.

"Ersi. Put the knife down. Let go of my XO. Now."

"Ask her why she turned the terraformers on."

"I mean it. We can talk about anything you want, but put the knife down and let her go."

"Three people are already dead. And you want me to let her go?"

"Yes, Ersi. Let her go. Put the knife down."

"Why aren't you asking yourself why she did this?"

"Because I didn't, you psycho freak." Kal sputterred.

"Whoa, Kal. sh. Ersi, stop. Now. We can talk but not like this."

"Don't you care about anyone on this crew? Or the colonists?"

"Of course she does." It was taking all she had to keep Dae from advancing.

"That's a temple over there. And what's in it couldn't be made accidentally. She's controlling all this. And I think you know it."

"Fuck you, you fucking abortion."

"Kal, stop it. Fuck. Ersi. look at me. Stop this."

"And you won't do anything to stop this. Nothing. That's why it has to be me."

"So you just want to kill us all?" Dae moved right. I could see she was trying to surround her. The problem was we were just a tiny bit too far away. I couldn't cover that distance before she stabbed Kal."

"You know you don't want to kill anyone. That's not who we are."

I looked down and the space around me began to swirl. There was a translucent cyclone shape forming between us as the space expanded. Was there another wave of terraforming happening?"

The sun shimmered and blinked and suddenly it felt like Ersi and Kal were on a treadmill moving backwards. I tried to keep my footing.

"Ersi! Stop. Don't do this."

"Tell her to stop it!"

'I'm not doing anything. I didn't do this."

"You lying bitch." I could see the knife in her hand rising over her head. I started running but I was barely covering the expansion between us. I yelled for her to stop by it didn't do any good.

Kal screamed as the knife blade came down over and over, hacking at her neck. At first, it seemed like it was a fake blade. She fought back. But within seconds a rope-like ring of red wrapped itself around her neck, choking her, while the clone pulled her hair upward. She dropped the knife and dug her right hand into the space in her neck as Kalista slowly stop struggling.

And ripped her head off of her body.

"Noooo." I fell forward and it seemed like the ground rose up and slapped me in the face. I saw Dae fall to my right while the grass shifted and flowed in front of us like water, pouring into a trench that had cracked open in the earth between us and the clone. Kal's body twitched for a second on the ground and then laid still as Ersi fell forward into the chasm holding her blood-soaked head still by the hair.

I crawled up and screamed after her, watching the earth heal between us like an accelerated incision, firming and solidifying as rain began to fill the space in front of me. I made it to Kal's body before I felt an impact in the back of my head that sent me into blackness.

-4 days

My left foot slipped into the pool onto the steps leading downward from the blue tiled deck. I pulled back as the poly cover advanced. In my head, I've tried to do the math over and over again for how long I could have tried, how long I could have worked to stop the cover from closing and saved a life.

The numbers never add up. It never makes any sense. And every night I have that dream, I lose again, sometimes pulling out, stepping back, and watching the water fill with death from my safe area above.

But every once in a while, I miscalculate, and I slide under the cover myself, watching it inexorably crush the intervening space, docking into a thin groove in the far wall over my head while my lungs fill with water and I feel the supernova in my chest burning hotter and hotter, building until I'm forced to take a breathe, sucking water in through my teeth, invading my throat like cement, sealing my lungs into two solid balls, pulling me down to the pool bottom where I can watch the slow Ink scrawl of death from the other side.

And I die.

But not today.

I felt Dae's hands around my head, holding me up over the surface of the water, pushing me toward the far shore.

I sputtered and came to life in her hands. We were barely floating in a marsh while the sun sank behind a mountain range clearly visible to our left. None of this was here before I was knocked unconscious.

"What...?"

"The trees behind you started falling, dropping branches and one knocked you out. That whole area is different now. And there have been two more expansions.

"How long was I out?" The rain was lighter than when I blacked out, but still pouring down. Where was it coming from?

"I don't know. Maybe an hour? I've been trying to get to the dry field for the last fifteen minutes."

"Where is Kal? Kal's body? Where is it?"

"I'm not sure. I was trying to keep us all together but this is unstoppable."

"So, no body?"

"We saw it. We saw what the clone did."

"I'm not believing anything until I see a body. All of this could be some kind of hallucination."

"Ok, I'm with you." We pulled ourselves onto the slightly dryer land next to the marsh. "What next? Do we go back?" she yelled over the rain, louder than needed.

"No. We find and restrain this fucking clone. Nothing's changed. We find our people if they're alive. Then, we turn these fucking machines off if that is, actually, what is happening."

"I'm in. But where is she?"

"If she's smart, she'd be holding up until this rain is over. And there is one place she knows nearby."

"That temple."

"She knew what was in it. She confronted us as we approached it. I think there's something in there."

"Ok. ok. Hold on. One second." Dae stopped and screamed.

Her shoulders hunched and she sank into herself. I watched her hair plaster itself to her face in the rain and she looked small - smaller than I'd ever seen her.

"Just hold on. Over the last twenty four hours I've watched two of my best friends die. I almost watched you... This is... I don't understand.Why is she doing this?"

I reached out to hold onto her. "I don't know. I don't know any more than you. I'm on pure adrenaline right now. If I stop, I don't know if I could get back up. She can't be a clone of me. I could never just do - that."

"What if you felt like it was the only way to carry out the mission? What if it meant life or death of over seventeen thousand people?"

"I don't know. And I don't know that anyone is dead. I need bodies in front of me. I need all of this insanity to wind down and to see what's left standing."

I could see the temple ahead of us with the unaided eye. Still not close, but not unattainably far.

"I've seen hundreds of these alien animals now. None of them are targeting us."

"Yeah, Only Kal. I saw that."

The terraformers were keyed to her. She was the only one who could really use them. Is that a coincidence?"

"There is no way she intentionally did this. I'd stake my life on that."

"I know, but I can't make sense of any of this."

"Let's hope there are answers there."

I pointed to the temple and we continued. For the rest of the time it took us to get there I honestly didn't know what to say. I know this wasn't what she signed up for.

The rain got steadily worse. By the time we reached the front of the temple we were soaked. And the winds had picked up dramatically, requiring that we make our way inside quickly.

THe temple front was made of metal. It was definitely a man made structure, solid and sturdy, with a precisely machined door in the front surface. But the surface was rough and covered with ridges and wires, bumpy and uneven. I tried to find a pattern but there seemed to be none. I didn't want to think too hard about what it looked like. The fact that it was there at all was a big enough conundrum.

What WAS this doing here?

Dae and I took our knives and began prying at the door. The door looked like it had been recently opened which filled me with hope. The clone could be in here. With answers, hopefully.

There must have been a sensor because the door slid open easily once we had moved it a few centimeters. We pushed our way inside the darkened space and let it slide shut behind us.

I tried something, thinking there was no way it would work. I hadn't been able to access the computer for hours. "Computer, lights on."

The lights blinked on, starting right above us and trailing down a long hallway. Within a minute or two it was entirely illuminated.

I looked at Dae and she shrugged.

"Computer, where are we?"

"You are in the engine room of the Veda Ecko 6, Captain."

"Ok, so where is the engine, computer?"

"You will find the engine one hundred and twenty meters ahead and to your right, Captain."

Dae looked concerned, "Computer, is the integrity of the shielding for the engine intact?"

"The shielding is intact, Engineer Park, and safe for you to approach."

We moved down the corridor. I put my hand against the leftmost wall. My head was telling me it was port, but it didn't FEEL like we were on a ship anymore.

Until we opened the door.

The room spread out ahead of us must have been about fifty meters by fifty meters. Teh ceiling was roughly the same size. And in the center was a ball, seemingly made of wires and metal globes wrapping around it. At first I didn't recognize it. Until Dae spoke up.

"It's Proxima B. It's the planet. A statue, something. That's not an engine."

The other side was dark. And something was over there.

We started moving around the sphere.

"Ersi. Is that you? Come out here."

"Be careful." Dae tried to keep up, but I wanted answers a lot more, I suspect.

"Is that you?"

"Zoo, it's me."

I saw her. It was Kal.

"Oh, my god." I started rushing to her, in the darkness. She pulled back.

"You didn't bring it."

"Bring what, Kal?"

"My body. Where's my body, Zed?"

"I don't understand."

"Did you leave it? To Die?"

Dae started moving toward her, "But Kal, you're alive."

"Did you leave me to die?"

I could see her hair now, moving into the light. She was crying. Blood pooled on the floor and a slow sucking sound filled the room.

"Why did you leave me to die?"

It was then I saw it. It was Kal's head, still ripped and bloody at the neck, on top of a three meter tall worm.

A nematode.

She was bent over, slithering toward us.

"Fuck, Kal. I'm sorry."

"Why did you let my body go?"

Dae tried to move forward to get her. I held her back. "We can get it, Kal. I'll go back and get it. I just couldn't find it."

Kall rose up to her full height. She was many meters tall and as she lifted her head i could see. Her face was missing. And in place of a mouth, a raw and ragged cut opened up. Blood spit from it with every word, uniting in a steady stream with the tributary of blood and pus leaking from the bottom of her head. None of this was possible.

'You BITCH!" Kal lurched forward and blood sprayed across us. Her lower worm half was surprisingly agile as she spun around the sphere. I jumped in the way and she swatted me to the wall with her tail like I was nothing as she pulsed toward Dae.

I felt my back crack as I hit the wall, forcing the air from my lungs. I tried to get up. I turned toward Dae, who was running from the giant worm that was once my best friend.

I reached up to steady myself on the wall and a hand grabbed mine to pull me up.

"You. Stop this." I pushed Ersi away, She moved into the light and I saw her.

She was all grown now. She was the same age as me. She looked identical to me now, even wearing the same uniform. But while mine was dirty and torn, hers was somehow pristine, new.

"I can't stop it, Mom. This isn't me."

"Don't call me mom. Don't manipulate me."

"Don't you think I would make everything go back to normal if I could. We need everyone for the mission. And look."

She pointed at the sphere. In her rampage to catch Dae, Kal was spinning into it, causing iit to wobble. Wires were falling from its surface.

"Don't you care about this mission? About this planet?"

"That's not the real planet. You need to stop this before Dae gets hurt."

"Everything matters more to you than the mission, mother. That's why you need ME."

She slapped me across the face. I fell toward the sphere and looked up. It was coming apart. But I couldn't focus on that now. I tried to get Kal's attention.

"Kal. Here. it's my fault. Stop it."

Kal turned her head and roared through her ripped mouth. It opened wider and suddenly her entire head came open, in two pieces. She was becoming more worm by the minute.

"Mother, that's not her anymore."

"I can reach her."

"No you CAN'T" Ersi grabbed my arms and pulled me away from Kal's descending head.

Why did she save me?

"Mother!"

"I'm not your mother." I looked toward Dae. Kal was advancing on her, leaning down. She was seconds away from wrapping her mouth around her.

Ersi grabbed the knife from the ground.

"Yes, you ARE"

She ran to the base of Kal's Nematode form and Jumped up, using the Knife to dig into her back, climbing her clumsily until she reached the top. She held on tightly as the Kal-worm bucked, stabbing her hand into the smooth aqua skin of it over and over. As she reached the top, she lifted her head and bit down hard where the head connected to the worm-like body of the creature, ripping and feeding on it like a predator.

Kal screamed and bucked, undulating, ignoring Dae. Seeing my chance, I ran to her and dove onto her, throwing her onto the ground. From there it looked even more surreal. Ersi held on to Kal's back, riding her like a bucking bronco as she clawed and bit, severing her head for the second time.

The worm exploded like a bag of blood hitting the ground and Ersi fell on top of it, still breathing hard, savage, animal like. She reached over to support the sphere.

"Help me, Mother. Both of you. Help me."

Without thinking, Dae and I ran to the base of the sphere to hold it steady, to keep it from falling. Moment by moment, it steadied.

Ersi was covered in blood, manic. I checked on Dae and the clone descended on me, pushing me against the wall. She seemed impossibly strong. Stronger than me.

"Do you see what I did? What I was prepared to do. You were willing to let the whole planet fall."

"That isn't the planet."

"You don't have a clue what's what. And you're not prepared to do what it takes to finish this mission. "

"So you have to take over? That's why you've been killing the crew."

"Goddamnit. I'm not killing them. You're letting them die. And you keep forgetting every time you learn what you need to do."

"I'm not forgetting anything."

"You're forgetting EVERYTHING."

She punched me and I used the inertia to slide to one sound, out of her grasp. I pushed her and she fell backwards. Dae stepped over her and held out her knife.

"Stop it. Now. Stop."

"And you. You don't even belong here."

Dae looked at me. Hearing her own fears coming out of the clone's mouth was powerful and it hit her hard.

'Why is she saying that?"

"Because she'll say anything right now to take over and get rid of me."

"Is that what you think? I'm not trying to get rid of you. You're going to die on your own. I'm just trying to get you to let go. Let go and let me take over."

The clone slowly started to stand. "Aren't you tired?"

"Stay back. I can't let you take over. You're a child. You're less than two weeks old."

"Do I look like a child to you?" She jumped up to a standing position. I couldn't have done that, even under the best of circumstances. I suddenly DID feel tired. I was beaten down. I couldn't even remember the last time I'd really slept or eaten.

The clone pulled her uniform top off and stood there in a white bra. She wiped the blood and sweat from her face with her top and threw it to the ground. She was dark and toned and muscular. She looked so alive, so fit and powerful. Had I ever looked like that?

"This is simple, Captain. Step down and let me finish this mission the right way."

"How. we don't even have a crew left. What are you going to do on your own that I can't?"

"Do you know what a Xenodrill is?"

I looked at Dae and she shook her head. The things she was saying, they sounded familiar. They made sense, in a way. I just needed time to process.

"Wait. one minute."

"It's a special set of routines established by NASA almost thirty years ago. A series of mental challenges that force the candidate to address and transcend their conceptions about the nature of the universe."

"I think I know."

"They push the candidate through Xenological situations, ones so alien and outside their frame of reference that it perverts their very understanding of reality. A mental exercise, really, that forces the candidate to evaluate and re evaluate everything they know to see how fluid they can think and problem solve. The candidate must - "

"Stop calling me the Candidate. I'm the captain of this ship."

"Really, mother, are you? Does this look like your ship to you? Does any of this look familiar? Does any of it look reasonable? Do you believe any of it is possible?"

Dae moved forward to hold my hand. "She's fucking with you."

The clone became enraged, "Why don't you just shut the FUCK UP. You're not even here. You're a figment of her imagination, something she uses to avoid doing her FUCKING JOB."

"I'm doing my FUCKING JOB."

"Is that really what YOU think is happening?" You're doing such a great job? How is your crew doing? How about the planet?"

She pointed to it. The yelling was causing it to shake again, sloughing off wires and gears, tiny spheres. It really didn't look like a planet.

"Does that look normal to you?"

"I just need to catch my breath."

"What makes more sense? The idea that terraformers are changing the shape and makeup of the ship on the inside while it stays exactly the same on the outside? Or that you are in a bed, experiencing a Xenological drill - one that you are FAILING badly?"

"You're the one yelling, making the planet - "

"Is that what you think it is? Does that really look like a planet to you?"

I looked up at it. Dark metal and chrome, ridges, wires, undulating waves across its surface. It looked familiar. But I couldn't see it. I couldn't remember.

She was right. I WAS forgetting things.

I reached for Dae's hand again. She stood there, beaten. Suddenly I realized that this idea- the idea that she didn't belong here- this was toxic. It was killing her. The very idea that she shouldn't be there was like a poison in her head, in her...

I looked up. It wasn't a planet.

It was a brain.

It was my brain.

And it was time to end this mess.

I advanced on the clone, grabbing her by the neck. I could see the surprise in her face as I pushed her backward, against the sphere. I charged and slammed her into it.

And it exploded as though it were held together by too taught rubber bands. I shielded my face as the wires and metal pieces went flying across the room, filling it like tiny insects cascading to the ground.

Metal shot out behind the sphere, ripping through the far wall and exposing what was right behind it, a brightly lit metal-clad room with the back of a couch spanning the space.

It was the Den of the Ship.

-1 days

The three of us sat at the table in the Galley. Ersi was tied to the chair at the far end of the table. The room felt the same as it always did, except it was empty, sanitized, Everybody's personal effects were gone. There were none of the upgrades that Ro had made. Kal's cooking supplies, Marin's knick knacks, the glasses that Kal had brought n ship from her own collection.

The computer had verified for us that there was no upper deck anymore, or Keel deck. The Pods were all gone and there was no longer a medbay aftward beyond the far wall of the lounge. The Den was the only part of the ship that we could see, feel, or access. The doors to each side that led to the corridors were gone now, as was the stemway stairs that led down, along with the transom way and every part past the Lounge.

We were on a ship that, if it were real, had no real method of locomotion, no struts or landing features, no engine room, no storage and no place for people to live or sleep. The most remarkable thing, though, is that it looked as though this were totally normal.

And the way it always was.

Dae pulled at the cords restraining the clone. There was no way she was getting out of that.

So I made sandwiches.

"Ok, little one. If this is really some kind of xenodrill, how come it's still running? True answers only, lies mean no sandwich for you."

I looked across at her. She did look smaller now. A little. It was still amazing, though, how much she looked like me.

"I could give you all the answers again, but you would forget them, again, and we'd be right back here."

Dae grabbed a sandwich from the plate. Through it all, the bread was fresh. I felt like there might be a commercial in there somewhere.

"That's called 'gaslighting,' when you try to convince the other person that THEY are the crazy one and that's why you are acting crazy."

"I know what it's called."

"Look, we don't know how you know ANYTHING. You have never told us the truth about anything. So I have no recourse but to think you are an idiot."

I didn't think that was going to work. And it didn't.

"I'm telling you the truth about everything."

"I'm just forgetting."

"That's right."

"No sandwich."

"You don't get it."

"So tell me again."

"She's not real. She doesn't belong here." She nodded at Dae.

"Ok, this is starting to hurt my feelings."

"It's not me saying it, it's crazy clone over there."

"But she looks exactly like you. It hurts."

"You continually put her ahead of the mission."

"So you say. Like I put the other crew members ahead of the mission."

"Yes."

"So you had to kill them, one by one."

"I didn't kill anyone. Your stubbornness did."

"All of this was you."

"I'm not real, either."

"Wait, this is new. So what are you?"

"Once you let me take over, I'll be you. And I'll finish this mission. There are over seventeen thousand people on their way RELYING on us. And you don't care. But I DO."

"Of course, I care. I left my home forever to do this. I left almost everyone to be here."

"Who did you really leave? You have no one who isn't here."

"Don't let her rile you up, Zoo."

"No, let it rile you up. You SHOULD be riled up. When that ship shows up and you haven't completed the mission and they're all dying on some alien world, you SHOULD be riled up."

"Jesus."

I shoved a sandwich in her mouth. Trying to eat that without her hands should keep her occupied for a bit. I grabbed Dae's hand and we moved to Helm control. I thought I would try this again, although I didn't have high hopes for any different outcome.

"Computer, how is this ship moving?"

"The ship itself is not actually moving, Captain, but is encased in an Alcubierre bubble that is both at motion and stationary in a spacetime that is folded, with the space in front shortened considerably and the space behind extended. This allows…"

"Ok, computer. How is that happening without an engine?"

"I do not understand the question, captain."

"Computer, do you know what an engine is?"

"Yes, captain. An Engine is a machine that converts energy into mechanical power or motion. The most common types of engine are.."

"Ok, computer. Hold."

"Zoo, it's like it can only respond to conditions in THIS version of reality."

"Which is not really one we are used to."

"Do you think it's really a test?"

"That depends. Is it a test that you're in, too?"

"Well, I've been thinking about that. Maybe we ARE in a test and it's a shared sort of cognitive space- like a device that generates Beta waves that can be shared. We are both asleep on some couch somewhere."

"And maybe I'm just a brain in a vat."

"I was thinking that. This is a classic philosophical thought experiment."

"It is either a test or it is really happening. In either case, the objective is the same."

"Right, but some of the parameters might change."

"MIGHT change. We have no idea. Honestly, we have so little understanding of the parameters that it makes no sense really to behave differently one way or the other."

"So if this is a xenodrill, or whatever, as you squared over there says, we do things the way we would ordinarily?"

"That's what I'm thinking."

"Good talk." I kissed her on the forehead. Dae grabbed my hand.

"Wait. one more thing."

"Yep." I turned back to her.

She stared at the clone through the doorway. "Since she got caught back at the temple, she hasn't called you 'mom' or 'mother' once."

"So no more trying to manipulate me?"

"Not that way, at least."

"Got it."

According to the computer, we only had twelve hours to go before we were in orbit over the planet. Somehow we had lost time in the 'simulation' and the trip was nearly over. Luckily, there was nothing for a crew to do when landing. It's entirely possible, too, that the parts of the ship currently missing could be accessed from the outside of the ship which seemed to have maintained its original shape. The wraparound helm control window let us see parts of the ship that had not been maintained in this new manifestation. Looking to port, for example, you could see the start of port steerage, which was personal storage facilities.

The outside of the ship, at least what was visible, was the same as it had always been, visually confirming our earlier experiments.

If what was in the storage bays of the ship was intact, it was very possible that the two of us could manage much of what we needed to do. I considered for a minute what to do with the clone and realized that if I wanted a permanent solution for that, I should hurry.

I'm not a killer. And certainly without knowing what was actually happening. If this were entirely a simulation, maybe it would end once we met the criteria of the mission. Again, one way or the other, accomplishing the mission was the move.

At that moment, an alarm went off. I looked around the helm and called out, "Computer, what is that alarm?"

"Captain, that is an alert for extraction"

"Extraction? What does that mean? Can you turn it off?"

"Yes, Captain." The alarm silenced. But the swirling red lights continued.

"What is that?"

"Is the clone still there?"

"Just sitting at the table."

I stepped into the Galley. She looked up at me.

"What is an extraction alarm? That's not standard."

The clone laughed. "Ha. You'll see."

"Sonofabitch. What is an extraction alarm?"

"Untie my hands and I'll tell you."

"No. Fucking burn. I don't care."

"Don't you want to know?"

"I don't want you running free on my ship, you fucking lunatic."

"It looks to me like you are running out of ship."

"I think we should untie her. She can't really do much. What are you going to do, cut her arms off?"

"That is a great idea."

"Seriously."

The red lights of the alarm continued. I took a deep breath.

"Fine." I roughly untied the clone's hands. "What is that alarm?"

"It's the extraction alarm."

"Yes, what is being extracted?"

Ersi pointed to Dae. "Her."

"Fuck you." I was sick of this garbage clone. I grabbed the rope.

"No, wait. It's ok. She's not real. She's not real."

"Nop, seriously, fuck you," Dae shot back.

"You need to get her off the ship."

"You want me to throw her out of the ship?"

"Not me, the ship. That's what the ship wants. To extract her."

"Bullshit."

"You don't get it. None of this is real. This is a test. It's an exercise. Are you willing to put the mission ahead of her?"

"No. I'm not willing to kill anyone. Except maybe you, if you don't stop."

"Go ahead. I'm not real, either. I'm just waiting to be you when you give it up."

"Why would I do that?"

"Take a look at the helm."

I turned to the helm control and looked through the door.

The red alarm lights illuminated cracks appearing on the front window in helm control.

"What happens if those cracks open up?"

"How are you doing this?"

"I'm telling you it's not me. But you have to get rid of her. Let her go."

"Zed. This can't be my fault, is it?" Dae looked back and forth between our identical faces.

"The clone is lying."

"I don't want to die. But I don't want to stop the mission. What do I do?"

"You aren't leaving the ship. That's suicide."

"Put me in there."

"What?"

"In the helm control area. Then block it off. Maybe it's ok if I just get off this main area. Then, if helm is compromised, I'm the only one that gets hurt."

"No, that's fucked up."

"If the helm is compromised, it could destroy what's left of the ship."

"I don't care."

"Do you really not care?" spit out the clone. "That's why I should be leading this. "

"Shut the fuck up." I wasn't going to put her in there, but blocking off the helm control was a good idea.

"Computer, fire protocol for helm control."

"Yes, Captain." The doors slid shut covering up our view of helm control. They should be absolutely structurally sound. They would hold even if the entire Helm exploded. "Transfer all extraneous control still in helm to the Galley."

"Affirmative Captain."

"Why did you do that?"

"I'm not putting you in there while the views are compromised. The entire area could explode outward.

"This isn't solving anything." The clone was really getting more annoying by the minute. I picked up a metal plate from the drawer next to the Galley table and brought it down hard on her head. The clone tried to raise her hands on time to protect her head but failed. She slid to the ground.

"Shit. That felt real enough."

"Holy. Did you kill her?"

"I'm still not killing anyone today. I mean, there really is no safe way to render someone unconscious, but I'm getting sick of my own voice and that can't be psychologically safe for me, so..."

A muffled explosion rocked the ship, drawing our eyes forward.

"Computer, identify that explosion."

"The view ports in Helm control became compromised and the entirety of helm control is now gone."

"That was quick."

"Jesus."

"I wasn't about to lose you that way."

"Computer, how long until we're planetside?"

"Approximately Seven hours, twenty minutes, Engineer Park."

"Dae looked at me. "This is fucked. This is why it doesn't feel real. We just lost almost five hours."

"Good, We need this to be over. We need to be planetside."

"You're hiding from all this."

"Dae, if all this is real, I just lost my entire crew, except you and an uncontrollable clone on an alien planet where no one will arrive for nearly a year. If it's a simulation, it'll be over in the next few hours and who knows what it will show. Maybe they're alive. Maybe Kal is and Ro, and Marin and Lyra. These are people who depended on me and I failed them."

"You didn't fail them."

"I did. I was the captain and I failed them."

The alarm kicked back in again.

"Goddamn it. Computer, is that the same alarm?"

"Yes, Captain, it is the extraction alarm."

"Computer, do you know what is supposed to be extracted?"

"Captain, I'm afraid I do not."

"I do." Dae pushed me away. "Computer, is the extraction alarm for me?"

The computer voice paused for less than a second, but it was long enough.

"Yes. Engineer Park, you are meant to be extracted."

"Computer how does that happen?"

"Dae, stop it. Cut it out. You aren't going anywhere. There aren't even any airlocks left on the ship."

"I have to go. This is the only way."

"You have to stop listening to this fucking clone." I looked down and realized that Ersi was gone.

"How is she gone?" Dae began looking around. What was left of the Den was only a few meters in every direction.

"Captain, you wanted audio confirmation about changes in the spatial integrity of the ship."

"Yes, computer."

"Captain, the Lounge is ten square meters smaller than the last time I made the evaluation."

I looked behind me. The back couch of the lounge was gone. The aft wall now was at least a meter closer.

"We won't land in time." Dae yelled over the alarms.

"Computer, can you kill that damn alarm?"

"Yes, Captain."

"We will. We're almost there. And what if all of this goes back to normal once we snap out of warp space?"

"Do you think that?"

"I don't know what to think."

"There is something exponential going on. What if the time to planet and space rmaiing ar on a path to a singularity. And we land, just as we disappear?"

"I have no reason to think that's the case."

"Captain, there is a structural instability in the port wall of the Lounge area about one and a half meters from the connecting ring to the main galley."

"Fuck this." I looked over the port wall. I couldn't see anything.

"Dae, do you see anything?"

"Nothing. No cracks. Nothing."

"Do you see the clone anywhere?"

"I do not. Where can the clone be?"

"Computer, mark the position of the clone of me."

"There is no clone of you on the ship, captain."

I was getting really sick of having a computer with no real connection to reality. THere was no way to know the things I didn't know were hovering, right outside my view. One way or the other, this clone would need to fend for herself.

"Computer, FIre door protocol between the Galley and the lounge." I moved to the table with Dae. One way or the other, we were going to make it planetside, even if it was in a one room ship.

"She's not here. The clone. She's gone."

"I can't say I'm really overly stressed about that. I need to get what's left of this ship down to the planet. With you in it."

"If we don't make it…"

"We will. We have to."

She kissed me.

"Computer, how much longer until planetfall?"

"Captain, there are thirty four minutes remaining until planetfall."

Dae put her arms around me. That's wrong. That's so wrong. But I don't know what's real."

I looked at her. "So stay right here. No matter what. For the next thirty four minutes. In my arms."

"I'm not going to make it."

"Of course you are."

"I don't. Remember having a physical before we left."

"But you're ok?"

"Sure. but that's not the point. I don't remember signing up."

"But you did. You're here."

Dae started crying. "I don't think I am. I don't remember leaving on this ship."

"But I do. I remember you."

"Do you?"

Another muffled explosion shook the room.

"Captain. The lounge area of the ship has collapsed. The structural integrity of the Galley area has been compromised."

"Computer, please silence all alarms."

"Yes, Captain."

The room became quiet. Quieter than quiet, as though it was an inversion, a kind of super-silence.

I held onto Dae as tightly as I could. For a moment I thought about what NASA would need to know about this mission. I tried to think of a way to relay all the way back to earth what had happened and why it had gone so far off the rails. But there was no way. I pulled her close and kissed her.

The galley swam around us, lights flickering and I pulled her face close to mine. There was no point looking, no point panicking, no point in anything anymore except holding on and descending to a planet that may not ever feel our footprints. I was glad we had gotten this close. I imagined our atoms merging with the atmosphere on the way down, becoming a thin photosphere of humanity wrapping itself around a planet that was going to welcome people soon enough in its own awkward way.

I thought about the colonists and how many would live, even without our physical help and what they would think about us, absent in every way except for our intent to be here and help, impotent as every angelic guarding had ever been throughout history, but watchful, like ancestors, as their story took over our own.

I closed my eyes tightly and kissed, giving Dae all the breath i had left as the world around me went black and dissolved into a whole new one.

Zero

My bedroom back in Austin had stylish black walls, filled with green accents and plants. The bed was spartan with black and green sheets. One side was filled with extraneous pillows and randomly colored blankets.

Dae's side.

I slid out of bed. I was in a pair of underwear and nothing else and I could feel the floor warmers kick in as I rested my full weight on the floor and padded over to the window. It looked to be about Nine am. Past the manicured lawns and fences I could see the street. Austin Texas. Pulling the window open I inhaled. The smell of cut grass and Mexican food from the restaurant two doors down met the sounds of people, children.

People laughing.

I was home.

There were so many people outside. Even in my rarified neighborhood, the beat of overcrowding was audible. The sounds, the smells, the weight of human excess. People were everywhere.

Earth.

"Hey, baby." Dae was in her underwear, carrying two cups. She handed me one and, in one easy motion pulled off her bra like she did nearly every time she walked into the bedroom. The simple black bra sailed over to the bed and slid off to the carpet.

There were likely five or six bras under that bed by now. "No one's around, but the windows were open. I'm modest."

She kissed me and took a drink. I knew there was a sweet milky chai in that cup, just like I knew there was black coffee in mine, no sugar.

I'd lived this morning many times over.

"Dae?"

She climbed over the mound of pillows and sat crosslegged on the bed facing me.

"You don't remember, do you?"

I shook my head.

"It's ok. They said you'd forget a few more times before it settled in. It's ok. That's what the video is for."

I sat down next to her in the bed as she smiled and reached for my hand.

"Alba, play NS220 in the main bedroom."

My home computer responded. I remembered that I had named her Alba after a close friend of my mother's who had babysat for me. I tried to make her voice as similar as possible. It was a sweet, refined soprano, lilting and non threatening.

"Of course, Dae. And welcome back, Zedi. You were definitely missed around here."

"Thank you, Alba. What is NS220?"

"It's a recording that you made when you returned. You are currently experiencing slight Anterograde amnesia and may need some assistance in building new memories. Your employers believe that this recording may be of assistance until your brain recovers its full function."

I shifted uncomfortably and took a sip. "That sounds pretty ominous."

Dae kneeled on the bed and shimmied out of her panties, too. "It sounds worse than it is. You've been through a lot."

Alba paused, then asked, "Do you want me to continue?"

I reached for Dae's hand. "Of course, Alba, thank you."

The room darkened and the far wall sprang to life with a giant image of my face. For a second, in my panic, I imagined it as Ersi's face and pulled back. Dae patted my hand to comfort me and the face began.

"Captain Zedi Kimura, this is, well, this is Captain Zedi Kimura. In case it's not obvious, I'm you. And if it seems like I processed all this, be sure I have not. I recently heard it all for the first time. I've been told I'm forgetting things and this is the best way to address that in the short term, while my brain heals. You…I…We may have to play this every morning for a few weeks until we are healed enough for iit to sink in. But we've watched worse movies, so…"

I looked at Dae and she brushed the hair from my eyes. How many times had she seen this? Ten? Twenty?

You've probably noticed that you aren't on Proxima B. You are home, in fact, safe in your own home. And that goes for every member of your crew. The Eckospace Six mission failed but it was through no fault of your own or your crew.

It turns out that the Alcubierre bubble collects certain kinds of radiation and focuses it to the natural spacetime within, in cycles. Each cycle creates a health hazard that causes, among other things, memory loss and hallucinations. Shipboard records show that you and your crew began hallucinating less than four days out from Earth. And that you, well, we… I became incapable of command."

I looked down at my hands. This was a hard thing to listen to. But at least everyone was safe. The version of me in the recording seemed to send my discomfort.

"Nothing here is our fault. NASA has been making that really clear.

None of the nanoships were big enough to show this radiation and none were manned. This is something everyone learned a lot from. The behavior of the crew as they slid into their respective symptoms triggered a boomerang function that returned the ship home."

I looked over at Dae. This was news to me. All of it.

"Apparently they weren't sure it would actually work, so we were never informed about it. But it created an inversion of the warp bubble and brought the ship home like a slingshot. We landed and the radiation was siphoned from all of us."

"Alba, pause recording."

Dae put her cup down.

"Does this make sense to you, Dae? Does it seem real?"

She cocked her head, "Of course. I mean, everything just went crazy. None of it made any sense. It couldn't have been real, right?"

"I guess. This just seems so ... pat, you know."

"Well, sometimes life is just what it seems like."

"Are you going to get that on a t-shirt?"

"I think I will. Don't push me. I'll get little shorts with that on the ass."

"Alba, continue," I wanted to hear what I was expected to do now.

"Of course. Continuing."

The giant face on the wall went on.

"They sent a newly upgraded ship, with some new guinea pigs, and a drive buried in seven feet of metal. That will, apparently, work. We're supposed to be relaxing. The rest of the guys are being reassigned to short, temporary missions. We are scheduled to leave, full crew, all of us, in nine months, to Ross 128 B, which should take about a month and a half.

We will be preparing for the arrival of the Ever Frumious Bandersnatch 1, which left Earth about sixty freaking years ago, carrying mostly phone sanitizers. You and I get that joke. Nobody else. Dae has some work to do, but your job - our job, is relaxing. The logs are all uploaded so you are free to look at those. I did. They are boring. So, slightly future me, do me a favor. And just go to bed. We'll be up and out in nine months. That's an order."

The wall blinked out and the ambient lights in the room rose a bit.

"Can you just order yourself? Does that work?"

"Apparently. I'm a bossy little bitch."

"You're my bossy little bitch."

"So, hey, you have to head out? Did I hear that correctly?"

"Yes. But not for a few weeks. And I'm currently as naked as I can actually get. An opportunity? I think so. "

"I like it. But weeks, huh?"

She climbed into my lap and put her arms around my shoulders.

"It'll pass so fast. Then we'll chill, and then we'll go to this new discount planet and get jiggy."

"Is that something the kids still say?"

"Nope." she kissed me. I could feel her hands on me in all the familiar places, the comfortable things we did when we were alone.

It seemed like no time at all had passed. I know I must have watched that recording at least four times. Alba explained to me that my brain was healing but I still might lose time. It was frustrating. But I understood. Honestly, I was feeling better, although all that resting seemed to make me feel MORE tired. As I went with Dae to the hangar, I resolved to get up and exercise more.

With her leaving for a short time, I would certainly have the opportunity.

"Wait, how long are you leaving for?" The crowd around us was thick. It was mid afternoon, a busy time for travel.

"Zoo, we talked about this. Don't worry."

"Ok, yes, I forgot, I think, exactly. How long?"

"You keep forgetting."

"Yes, yes, I forget. I'm sorry. Just tell me one more time."

"Zed, I have to go. It's my flight." She turned around

"Please, Dae, humor me. How long?"

"Don't do this. Don't do it now. Just say goodbye. I'll call you tonight."

I grabbed her arm. Something felt wrong.

"Just tell me."

"Zed, you have to let go. You have to let me go."

"For how long?"

"Please, let me go. Why won't you?"

"Just tell me - "

"I'm gone. I'm dead, Zoo. You have to let me go."

"What?"

"Take your hand off. Let me go"

"What do you mean, you're dead?"

"In the pool. I died. In the pool. You couldn't stop it and now you won't let me go."

"You're not dead, you're right here."

"And you're dying. The radiation. The ship is malfunctioning. The radiation is killing you."

"But we landed." Did we land?

"Why can't you let the body take over for you?"

"Wait, Ersi? Is that what this is about?"

"You'll be dead in a few seconds, baby. And I'm gone. There isn't anything left to hold on to."

I saw the pool in my head. The number 6. The sixth pool. The clear cover slowly closing, and there she was, trapped inside.

"I couldn't save you."

"No one could save me."

The roar of the people fell away as I felt myself sink into the water on the steps of the pool. She was choking. Dae was dying and I couldn't stop it.

"How can you be dead?"

"You have to let go of it all. Let me go. Let your mind go. It's time you released us all"

"I can't," I held on to her arm. Her shirt disappeared and she was in her swimsuit. "I can't just let go."

I slammed my arm into the cover, over and over. I smashed it, cracking it. I began pulling the pieces of the cover off, the shards in my way. The people around me started paying attention. They hammered at the cover. They tore the pieces from over her head and I dove in.

I pulled her out of the water and pumped her chest on the side of the pool. The other people around us fell away as she looked up at me. Her eyes filled with tears.

"Please, my love." she whispered, "You have to let me go. I'm dead. And it's killing you.

"I can't. I won't. I won't let you die."

"If you hold on you can't finish the mission."

"That's insane."

"The mission, Zed."

Suddenly, she was standing over me, dressed in her uniform. "Don't you care about the mission?"

"I do. But how can I just let you die? I don't understand what's happening."

"You can't stop it." Dae pulled out a bag and placed it over her head.

"What are you doing?"

"I'm ending this." She tied the bag to her head and almost immediately I could see her eyes bulge. She was suffocating. Like she did in the pool.

"Stop it. Why are you doing this?"

I tried to crawl to her but I couldn't. The space kept expanding between us. Her body seemed to move farther from me with every lurch.

"Why can't you let her go?"

Ersi was standing to my right, floating just inches above the ground.

"Shut up, you bitch."

"I can't believe I'm this stupid. I can't believe you're me."

"I'm not you." Dae's face nearly disappeared as she moved even farther away. If I could take out Ersi, I might be able to stop this. I grabbed at her.

"You're pathetic. Just let her go." Ersi stepped on my fingers and I could see them shatter, blood spraying across the floor."

"No." I crawled a few inches forward. Holding my hand with care. It hurt. I looked up at Ersi. Dae was there, in her arms now, naked. "None of this is real"

"This is the only reality you have."

"Zed, just let go. Your body is dying. And I'm gone. But Ersi is strong and healthy. She can finish the mission. She can protect me." Dae kissed her deeply. They ran their hands over each other. "It'll be like we're still together. But you have to let me go. I don't need you anymore."

"This is bullshit. None of it is real. I don't let you go. I won't. I don't know what all this is or what she's playing at, but I've lost enough."

"You. It's always about you. Can't you see I'm better. I can do this. The mission will be finished." Ersi pulled out a macro axe and severed my arm. I felt it throughout my entire body. It was a fire that wouldn't stop. I screamed.

Dae laughed. "Do it again."

She lifted the axe and pulled it down, cleanly severing my other arm. The fires intensified, ripping through me like an electric force, burning through my muscles and leaving scorched holes behind. I stared up at them through the blood and tears filling my eyes. My peripheral vision narrowed and I saw Dae enter it, still nude, Ersi's hand on her shoulder. She knelt down.

"You don't even have arms anymore to hold me. You can't do anything. You couldn't stop it. It's not your fault. "

"Don't do this."

Ersi stood up behind her. She took the axe and slid it across Dae's throat. I screamed as I watched her choke and die on her own blood.

My doppleganger tossed her body aside and kicked me in the face.

"This is you. You made all this."

I saw her boot come down on my face again and again. I tried to protect myself, even lifting the phantom limbs that had replaced my severed arms. But with each stomp my vision thinned until all I could see was black.

When I woke up, my arms were still attached to me. I lifted my hand and it looked healthy, unscarred. I was in the Medlab of the ship. The light bore down directly into my eyes

"Ersi! How are you doing this?"

"Are you awake now, mom?"

"How is any of this possible?"

"I keep explaining to you and you keep forgetting."

"The amnesia."

"You forget every time."

"What are you trying to get me to do? Why not just kill me?"

"you ARE me, mother. I'm you. And only one of us can complete this mission."

"Where is Dae?"

Ersi walked into my vision, dimming the lights. She was wearing all white now. She was tall and beautiful and perfect. I looked down and realized that I wasn't healthy. My skin was bunched up and raw, covered in lesions. I coughed and spit up blood on my forearm.

"She is dead and you are dying." You are ghosts. Ghosts that are jeopardizing the lives of thousands of colonists."

"I want to finish the mission." I fell to my knees. It hurt. I hurt. She was right. I was dying.

"You CAN'T finish the mission. But I can. Look at me."

She was strong and alive. I felt myself growing even weaker.

"Computer," She raised her voice, "Show me the manifest of the

Leviathan."

"Yes, Captain," a stream of names flashed by on the wall of the medlab.

"Show me footage of LV3202"

"Accessing footage."

On the wall I could see a little girl, maybe ten years old. She looked like she may have been korean, with long dark straight hair. I stared up at her as she played in a tiny lab.

"This is Astra Kim. She's two months away from her eleventh birthday. Her IQ is off the charts and she wants to be an engineer."

"Like Dae." She looked so alive. And I was so tired.

"Just like her. She's smart and she's funny and full of joy. And she's going to need a world to live on- one that is ready for her."

"It's so hard." I pulled myself up and saw it. There was Dae's body on the forward bed. She was in her bathing suit bottoms, topless. It looked like the coroner had cracked her ribs. "It's so hard."

I started crying.

Ersi lowered her voice. "It's harder than anything. But you have to let her go. These are the people who need us. These are the people who replace us. And life moves on. "

"I have to let her go?"

"You do. You've carried this for such a long time."

I moved closer and held her hand. It was so cold. Her skin looked hard and unreal. Her lips were blue as I leaned in to kiss them. Her body looked wracked with pain. It looked broken, tortured. There was no peace in its death.

"I let you go. This is all pain and I let you go."

Her body began to shimmer and brighten. Suddenly it seemed to lose size in some not easily seen dimension. And it disappeared. My hand fell onto the bed.

"Are you satisfied?" I looked up at the screen as the girl Astra played, silent until it looped back to the beginning. She was beautiful. She was the future. This little girl was nearly here, nearly home.

"Now I need you to give it to me."

"What do you want from me, Ersi?"

"I have to take everything. I'm sorry. I know you think I'm a monster. But I'm what I have to be,"

"What do I even have left? I have nothing."

Her eyes focused upward.

I laughed, remembering the temple. "Ah. My brain."

"I need to finish the mission. I need everything you are to finish the mission."

I stumbled to the back of the medbay. Opening the drawer next to the Aft bed I pulled out a microlaser. I looked at Ersi and she nodded slowly. Her face, my face, always used to seem kind to me when I looked at it in the mirror.

Today, it was something else. I wondered how I could ever have seen that face - my face - as kind

I lifted the microlaser to my skull.

The last thing I remember is pulling the top of my skull free.

I never heard it hit the floor.

Day 30

I woke up in a slightly chilled clean white room with Lyra hovering over me. Kalista was in a chair by the window. The air smelled raw and medicinal, but fresh. The beeping from a machine to my right seemed to announce my eyes opening. Each beep fed like a tiny lightning bolt into the smooth rumble of the air around me.

"Hey, there, captain. It's about time." Lyra spoke loudly as though she were manufacturing hopefulness. Kal seemed to have the same instinct. Talk loud and everyone assumes it's all fine.

"Nice to see you up, Zoo."

"Is everyone ok?" a part of me was still panicking. These two were here, but what about the rest? What about Dae? I raised my hands to my head. Everything felt normal. My skin, everything.

Lyra looked to Kal. She had obviously been designated to explain all this to me. "I'm going to let you guys talk for a bit. I'll be back soon for some more tests.

"Thank's, Lyr."

"Mindfuck, I know." Kal sat on the edge of the bed.

I looked at lyra, leaving, "So, she WAS on the ship?"

"In a way. In a way we all were. This is weird because these are all things you would know. Things you SHOULD know."

"But I don't. I don't know anything. What's wrong with me? And where is Dae?"

"Ok." Kal looked around. She grabbed a sweater off the chair and draped it around me. "Let's get out of here. We can go check in on her."

I slid out of bed and stood up. I felt surprisingly good. I lifted my gown and looked at my inner thigh- the scar was gone. It felt surreal.

"Yeah. it's a clone body. Your original didn't make it."

"What happened to it, Kal?"

"Don't panic. It's all going to be ok, now."

We stepped into the hallway where Ro was sleeping in a chair outside the room, alive and intact. I couldn't believe how badly I needed to see him. I slipped my arms around him and he jerked awake. I held on to him tightly.

"Shit. Zedi. You're up." he jumped up and hugged me back, "Damn it's good to see you up."

"Yeah, Kal is just trying to explain what happened to me."

"Ha. how far did she get?"

"Not very." I looked at the window behind him and saw the sky. It was true.

"Yeah, we're here, Zed. This is Proxima B."

"How long was I asleep?"

Kal moved over to the window, "A bit. Not long. Less than a month." The sky seemed to be made of some kind of liquid reddish candy. All the colors were off, different, some the opposite of what I was used to seeing. There were no people. No one.

"How about you guys?"

"That's just it. We woke up weeks ago. Thanks to you."

"To me? What did I do?"

"Your overlay is a bit incomplete. We have to fill in some gaps."

"You think?"

Kal grabbed my hand and put his arm around me. I slid into the crook of his armpit. "Me, Ro, Lyra, Marin, our bodies are back on earth. Our minds were stored in yours as overlays so that we could be cloned here on the planet. They sent our DNA to automatically clone us."

"But, wait. The ship. What about the ship?"

Ro stood up. He looked out the window and pointed. I followed his hand.

"Do you see that?"

I saw it. A tiny ship, one that looked barely able to hold one person, sat docked among a few devices and generator type objects on the bay in front of the building.

"That can't be."

"That's the ship. You were the only living human aboard that ship. It was only for sixteen days. You were supposed to be put in a twilight state, with the personality overlay of four other people so that we could be cloned here on Proxima B. That's the Veda Ecko agenda. Engram - Consciousness Kinesthetic Overlay. ECKO."

Kal jumped in, " 4 personas plus the host. That's what human brains can hold. The extraction and reintegration systems were automated. They went to work the minute you landed."

"Wait. What about Dae? Where is she?"

Ro stood up. "Let's go see her."

Dae was in a room down the hall. The room looked exactly like the one I woke up in. She was still asleep. I felt her hand and it was warm, even in the slight chill of the antiseptic space.

"When does she wake up?"

Kal held her other hand, "soon, we hope. Lyra is working to make it so she accepts the overlay. Her body is a new clone. She's just out until the overlay takes."

"This is crazy. Her personality wasn't implanted in me?"

"It was. Just not. Well, not the same way."

Ro walked around the bed to hold my hand. "How much do you remember about what happened to Dae?"

"I had a, I guess a vision. Did you guys experience anything I did?"

"Everything, up until we were extracted. We were in your brain. We remember the trip." Kal laid her other hand on Dae's forehead to check her temperature. "We know that you didn't want to accept the truth."

I could feel it all inside me now. It was welling up. I could remember all the things Ersi said I was forgetting. I leaned against the bed.

"She died. In that pool. I remember." It was so clear now. It ran back through my head. Me, running to the edge of the pool. The white number six, enclosed in a circle. The see through barrier closing, covering the pool. It was so hard to look. I forced myself now. I saw the sleek blackness of her hair spreading like ink in the water as she suffocated and died.

Kal's eyes dropped. "You couldn't accept it. You did a brain scan. You had forty eight hours to transfer her consciousness into a brain to hold it. You found someone who could do it."

"In Isla Mujeres. I remember."

Ro continued, "and when the rest of us were implanted, the NASA team had no idea that you already had a personality implanted. Your brain was overloaded."

My stomach sank. "So I caused it?"

Kal shook her head, "No. You may have been able to carry all of us successfully, but the warp drive housing had a tiny crack. And it filled the cabin with radiation."

"Your body started dying from the radiation. Your brain, all of it. When the ship landed, the extraction and reintegration system interface -"

"Ersi." I remembered

"Yes. it only had fifteen minutes to get all of us out of your head before your brain died."

"Fifteen minutes?" It seemed impossible. Everything that had happened. Not sixteen days. Fifteen minutes. The whole trip.

"So it invented scenarios to get us all out of your brain. Some of them were apparently pretty brutal."

"To convince me to let go."

"You were holding on to the overlays so tightly. And it was crowded in there. You pushed the limits of your brain to breaking."

Ro provided a little timeline, "Lyra was the first one extracted and cloned. As the doctor, it was her job to assist on the rest."

"But the real Lyra Tambor is back on earth?"

"Exactly. She gave you your last medical checkup before you left. You remember that?"

"I do." Things were starting to become a little more clear. "So Ersi is just a computer program?"

"One designed to extract the personalities so that we could be cloned."

"Extraction and Reintegration System Interface."

"So what about Dae?"

"That's good news. You brought a doll with - a toy- that contained Dae's DNA. And her overlay was in your head."

"So why isn't she awake?"

Kal brushed her hair out of her eyes. Dae's breathing was so soft.

"We don't know."

We met up with Marin for dinner that night. He was in good spirits and he hugged me for a bit longer than was necessary. Everyone was grateful to me for carrying their brain patterns on the ship and no one seemed to blame me for the poor judgment of trying to save Dae.

Marin said she would wake up soon.

I hoped.

They laughed while we ate. And I might have, as well, if Dae were with us. This body felt good. I felt alive and powerful and ready to finish off the mission.

But I wasn't ready to laugh yet. Every day I woke up wondering if this was real. I remembered so many things that really didn't happen. What proof did I have that this was happening? I realized that none of us get that. None of us get iron-clad proof that what we think is happening is real. My case was just a little more obvious, more in the open.

Some days I wandered around, almost in a fog, waiting for the room around me to shift. I stopped believing that reality was really real. But with every new day came a new reassurance. The dreams began to go away. I wasn't on the side of that pool, staring through the clear poly cover into the black swirl of hair that meant death. I wasn't living through moments I couldn't stop in the night anymore.

And during the day, I had work that made sense. I used this new body to build things and test things and prepare for people that would fill this planet with sound.

We built playgrounds and schools for children. We built a movie theater for teenagers, who would slide their seats together twenty minutes into a movie they had no interest in and kiss for the first time, on a world their grandparents never even knew existed. And every day, I made this into reality.

And I hoped for things. And I hoped this was real. And after we'd built a city, I realized I didn't care if it was or not.

I only cared about one thing.

"Are the terraformers in place?" I walked with Kal and Marin through the halls of the assembly building. In places, I could still see the microbots smoothing out the junctures between the building's many pieces.

Kal puffed out her chest, "In place and working better than we hoped. It's insane. The air outside is actually breathable already, after less than three weeks. It's just not the right mix yet. And you should see the accelerated crops."

"I want to. How long until Leviathan gets here?"

"We have nearly a year still. And in a week, we should have our first reciprocating signal from Earth."

Marin was happier than I'd seen him, "I can't wait to talk to me."

Everyone laughed. I realized that I HADN'T seen Marin. I'd likely never met him before his consciousness was implanted in my brain. My only experience with him, on the ship, was in my fevered dream state.

I didn't know the real Marin. I made a point to fix that. Kal held my hand.

She had been there to check on me and Dae since we had been cloned.

He turned to me, "Captain, can I ask a question?"

It felt intimate, being alone on this entire planet with only five other souls on it. We were all there was here. And the building itself, the only one on the surface so far, built to house thousands of colonists, room after room...

Empty.

I nodded. This was a good time for secrets. This was the right time to anoint this new world with the blood of new truths. I winced thinking that. It was cringey.

"Sure. what is it?"

"None of us were in your head when you were extracted, at the end. But you seemed reluctant to let go. What finally made it possible for you to let go and let yourself be extracted?"

I had thought about this for a while. "I think that I let go of the thing that I had been carrying so long it became me. I just stopped. I let go of the guilt for not saving Dae."

"You couldn't have saved her." Kal recalled.

"No. But I needed to release the guilt of just watching her die."

"I was there, too."

"And you tried so hard. I watched you." I lifted her sleeve. The bullet mark was gone. We really were all released from the past.

And so did you. You DID try. It wasn't your fault."

"I had to let go of it all."

I thought for a second about Astra, the little girl coming in on Leviathan. I had looked her up in the ship manifest when I woke up. She was real. As real as anything could be.

Maybe I could introduce her to Dae.

On day thirty-five I walked outside. The air tasted mildly like fresh copper and it seemed like there was sooooo much of it. The oxygen levels were high and it was admittedly making me feel a little giddy. Kal explained that the terraformers were dramatically increasing oxygen levels and that this would level out as some of the other elements were introduced. Right now, the biggest risk was wildfires among some of the rapidly growing new flora. We kept watch, ready to become volunteer firefighters if needed. For the most part, I had little to do but build until the Leviathan landed. And then, my skills would be needed wrangling the colonists. As Captain I would be the defacto leader until the first election.

I had time to think about it, but it was a powerful idea. The very first free elections on a new world.

I visited Dae every day. Kal and I took turns staying in her room, talking to her, encouraging her to wake up. I hadn't had one of those dreams in a while and I was grateful. I wanted to look forward, not backward. I didn't want to fixate on the pool incident anymore and I was glad to see that anvil of guilt release itself. I just wanted to see her eyes open and feel the warmth of that smile again.

I knew that she would see the beauty of this new world even more readily than I did. She would respond right away to its cartoon-rich colors and massive, swelling lakes with their red waters, rich in Dunaliella salina, an algae similar to one found on earth, edible, nutritious, even, with a mild carrot-like taste.

She would get high from this slight overabundance of oxygen, a truth serum in doses like this, making you want to tell secrets and trust. She, of all of us, would treat this new world like a vacation spot, like a fresh resort untouched by tourists, and her laugh would prepare it for the children it would see within a few years, making the colonists not just displaced Earthlings, but true occupants of a new world, one that had no real name yet.

On day forty, I sat with Lyra to learn what I could of the medicine that we'd need to employ once the settlers arrived. I wanted to be useful and who knew how useful a captain would be amongst a group of civilians millions of light years from home. I had prepared myself for what they would need, but more likely than not what they would need was time, and space, and for me to get out of their way and let them learn how to live in a new place.

We had the chance to build a real paradise and if we couldn't do that, it would be no one's fault but our own. Everything we would ever need was here, on this planet, a world that had resources in abundance. We could choose how we wanted to live and how important we wanted to make simple human happiness. We could be a part of human history, not scribbled in at the end, apocalyptically, in the end of times, watching our world wind down, but a beginning, a new chapter, the start of a whole new book.

I thought about Ersi and forgave myself, because if we were going to have any chance of making things work here, we would all have to do that. We'd have to look at the different versions of ourselves in our heads and learn to love them just a little, and maybe get on the same page with them. My face, in the mirror, began to look kind to me again.

On day forty-two, I watched a new sun set on a new world with the only other people on the whole planet and got so drunk none of us could make it back to our rooms.

I stumbled to Dae's room and fell asleep to the regular rhythmic sounds of the hospital equipment monitoring her vital signs, feeling my heart sync to her heartbeat without even trying, curled up at the foot of her bed. I woke up in the middle of the night and nothing had changed.

I was there, where I had fallen asleep. It was all so expected and predictable and I loved it.

On day 44, I thought I saw her fingers move and I called Lyra who told me it was promising while she tried not to get my hopes up. I picked new flowers for her room and cleaned the dust off of the machinery and countertops.

The particulates from our constant construction had fallen everywhere, thick in the air in some places, like a veil to be pulled away when this new world was ready to be presented to its new owners. The air felt normal, real, earthlike, so I opened a window in her room.

Lyra scowled at me slightly but then thought better about reprimanding the captain.

Not in this room.

Not in her room.

And on Day 45, Dae woke up.

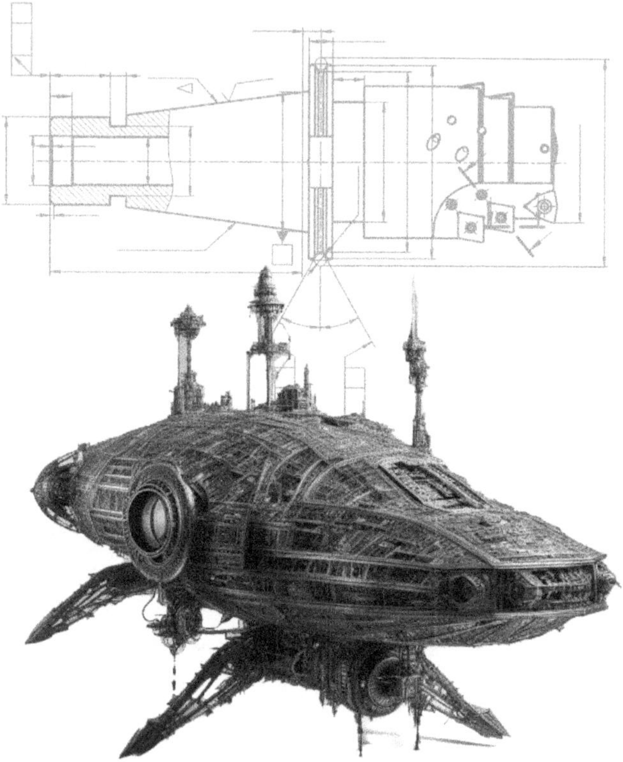

EKKOSPACE⑥

Veda ECKO 6

Engram-Conscious Kinesthetic Overlay
Alcubierre Drive Mechanics

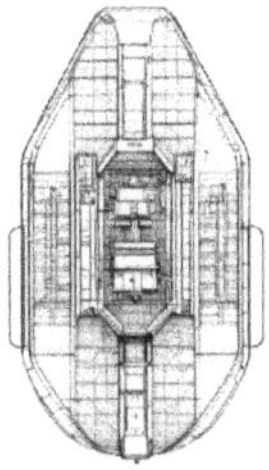

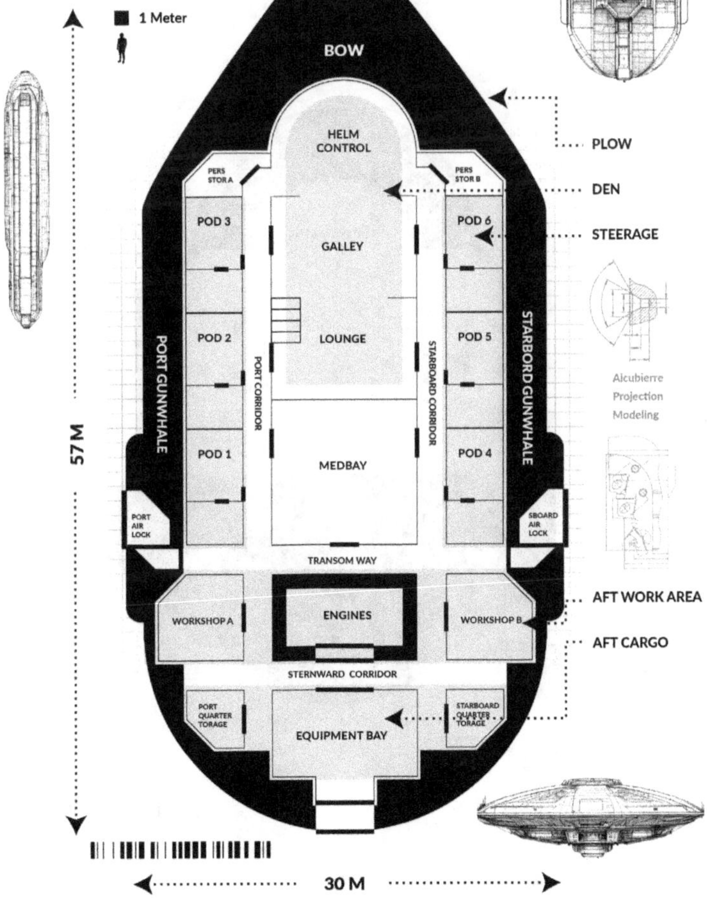

■ 1 Meter

BOW

HELM CONTROL

‹‹‹ PLOW

PERS STOR A

PERS STOR B

‹‹‹ DEN

POD 3

POD 6

‹‹‹ STEERAGE

GALLEY

PORT GUNWHALE

PORT CORRIDOR

STARBOARD CORRIDOR

STARBOARD GUNWHALE

POD 2

LOUNGE

POD 5

Alcubierre
Projection
Modeling

57 M

POD 1

MEDBAY

POD 4

PORT AIR LOCK

SBOARD AIR LOCK

TRANSOM WAY

WORKSHOP A

ENGINES

WORKSHOP B

‹‹‹ AFT WORK AREA

‹‹‹ AFT CARGO

STERNWARD CORRIDOR

PORT QUARTER STORAGE

EQUIPMENT BAY

STARBOARD QUARTER STORAGE

◄ · · · · · · · · · 30 M · · · · · · · · · ►

Main Deck
Primary Accomodations

2150

Veda ECKO 6

Engram-Conscious Kinesthetic Overlay
Alcubierre Drive Mechanics

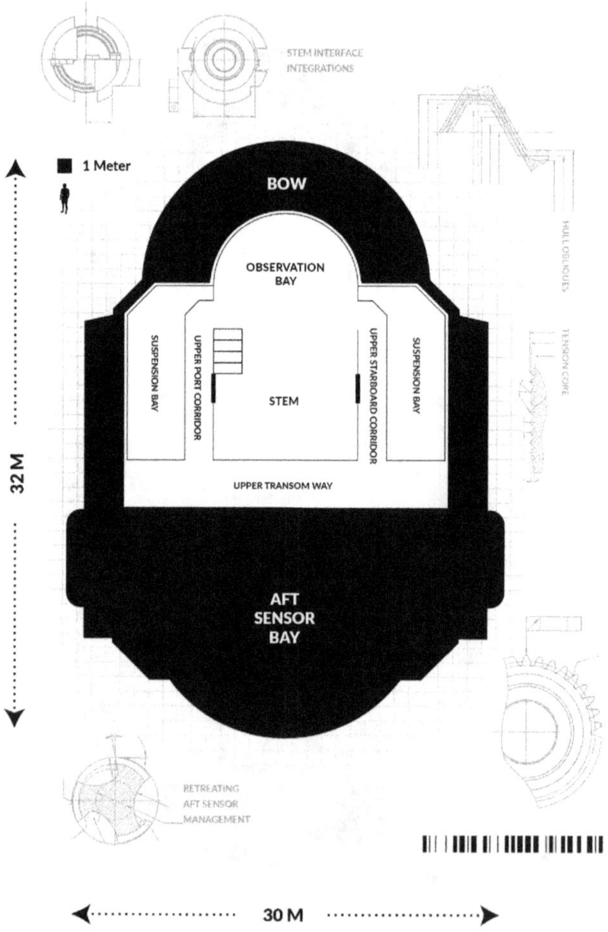

STEM INTERFACE
INTEGRATIONS
HULL OBLIQUES
TENSION CORE
1 Meter
BOW
OBSERVATION
BAY
SUSPENSION BAY
UPPER PORT CORRIDOR
STEM
UPPER STARBOARD CORRIDOR
SUSPENSION BAY
UPPER TRANSOM WAY
AFT
SENSOR
BAY
32 M
RETREATING
AFT SENSOR
MANAGEMENT
30 M

NASA
PRIMARY SPECS

Weather Deck

Topmost

2150

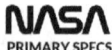

Veda ECKO 6

Engram-Conscious Kinesthetic Overlay
Alcubierre Drive Mechanics

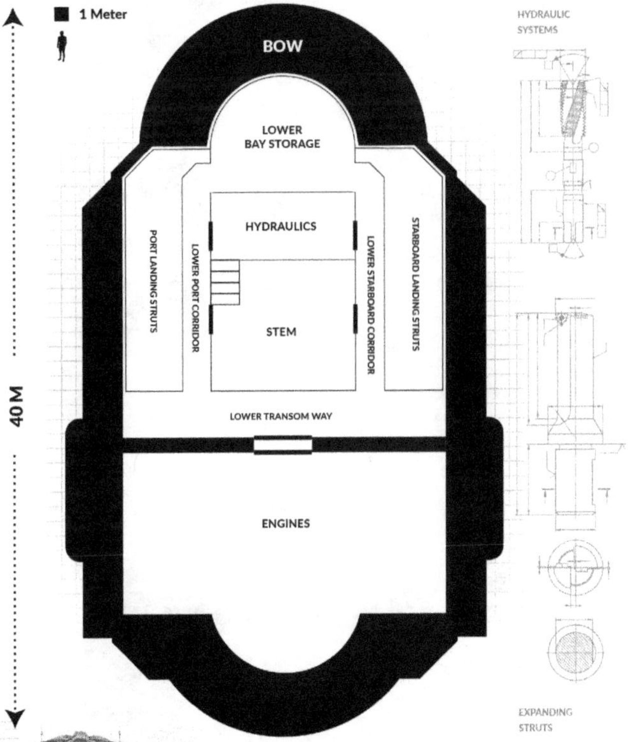
1 Meter
BOW
LOWER
BAY STORAGE
HYDRAULICS
PORT LANDING STRUTS
LOWER PORT CORRIDOR
STEM
LOWER STARBOARD CORRIDOR
STARBOARD LANDING STRUTS
LOWER TRANSOM WAY
ENGINES
40 M
HYDRAULIC
SYSTEMS
EXPANDING
STRUTS
30 M

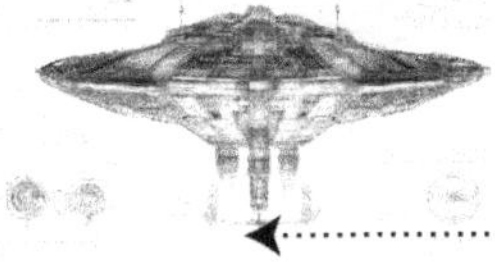

NASA
PRIMARY SPECS

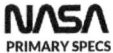

Keel Deck

Mechanics

2150

FIGURE 7

The Alcubierre drive achieves faster-than-light travel by stretching the fabric of spacetime, contracting space in front of it and expanding it behind, creating a warp bubble. The ship inside the bubble is carried along as the bubble moves, so it doesn't experience time dilation or violate the laws of relativity.

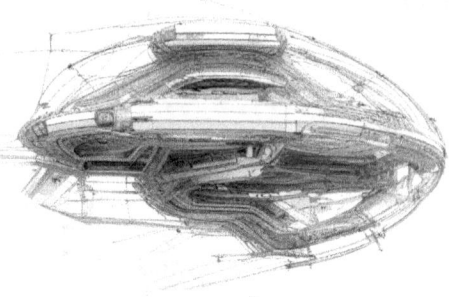

The spacecraft would be enclosed in a "warp bubble" of flat space and would not technically be moving itself so would not be subject to gravity or interia effects. It would arrive at its destination faster than light would in normal space, without breaking any physical laws.

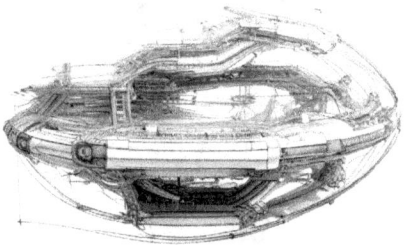

The Alcubierre drive requires the creation of a configurable energy-density field lower than that of vacuum, which is also known as negative mass.

Figure 12
Drive Bubble

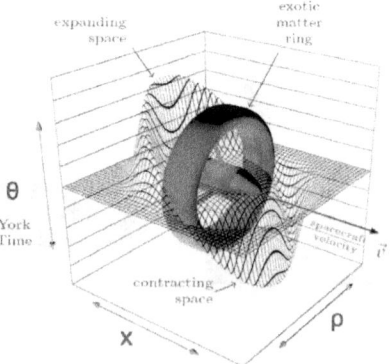

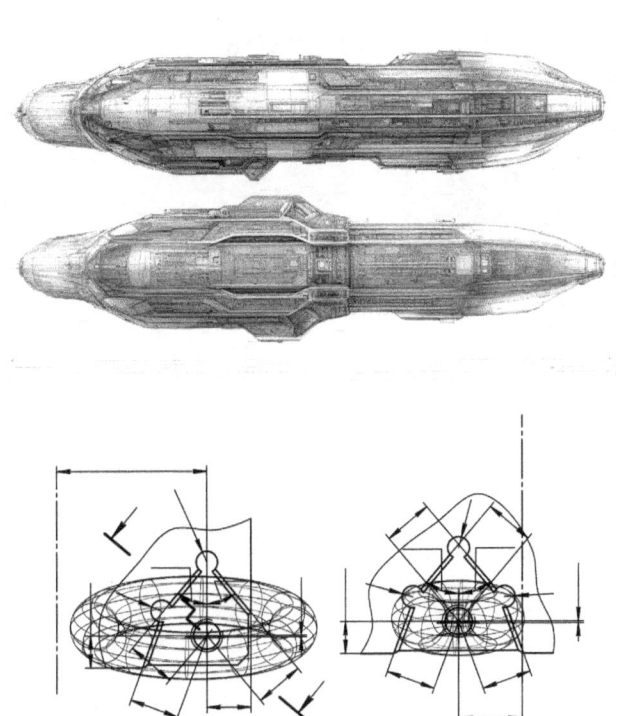

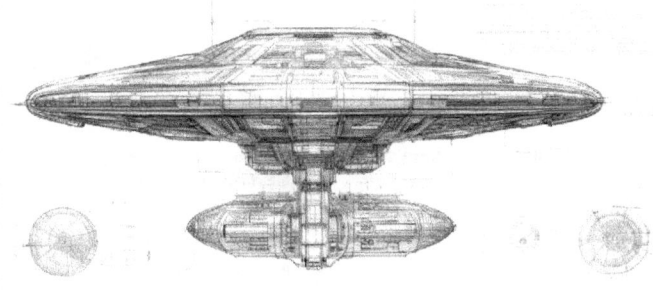

Alcubierre
Drive Mechanics

2150

Veda ECKO 6

Engram-Conscious Kinesthetic Overlay
Alcubierre Drive Mechanics

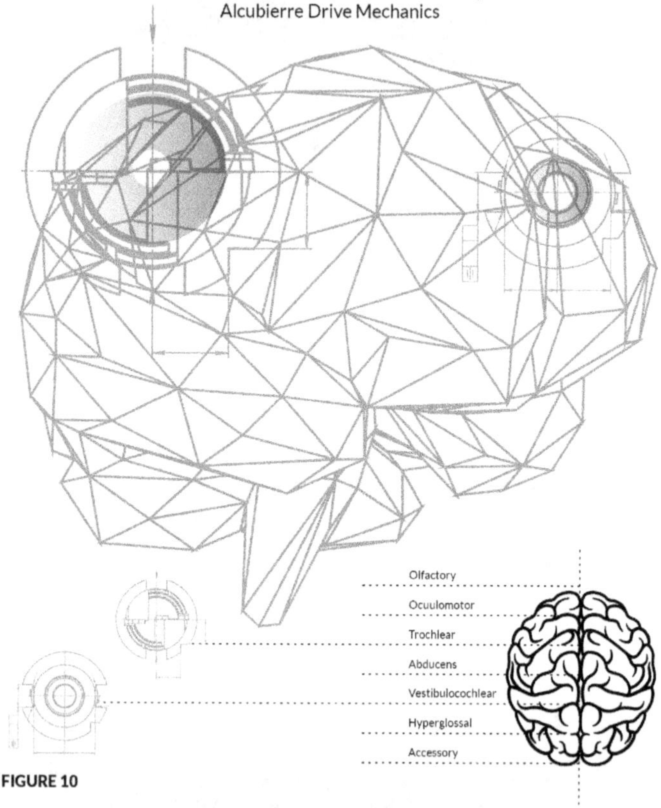

Olfactory

Ocuulomotor

Trochlear

Abducens

Vestibulocochlear

Hyperglossal

Accessory

FIGURE 10

The **Engram-Conscious Kinesthetic Overlay** creates a pool of talents that can be separated and refined into unique clone bodies on planetfall. The captain uses the interface to engage the skillsets en route and then the extraction occurs upon landing.

The **Extraction and Reintegration System Interface** is a secondary system that may be used to complete the process of rendering distinct agencies from the engram data. Both are available througout the trip but the latter is only engaged when needed.

FIGURE 12

The exoplanet Proxima b is 4.2 light-years away from Earth, and it is the centerpiece of our mission.

It is a super Earth, with a mass of 1.27 Earth, orbiting its star every 11.2 days, and is located in the star's habitable zone, where liquid water could exist.

The goal of an advance team is to initiate a forceful counterspin so that Proxima b is not tidally locked as well as managing satellite shield systems to mitigate radiation that could strip away the planet's atmosphere and any water present on its surface.

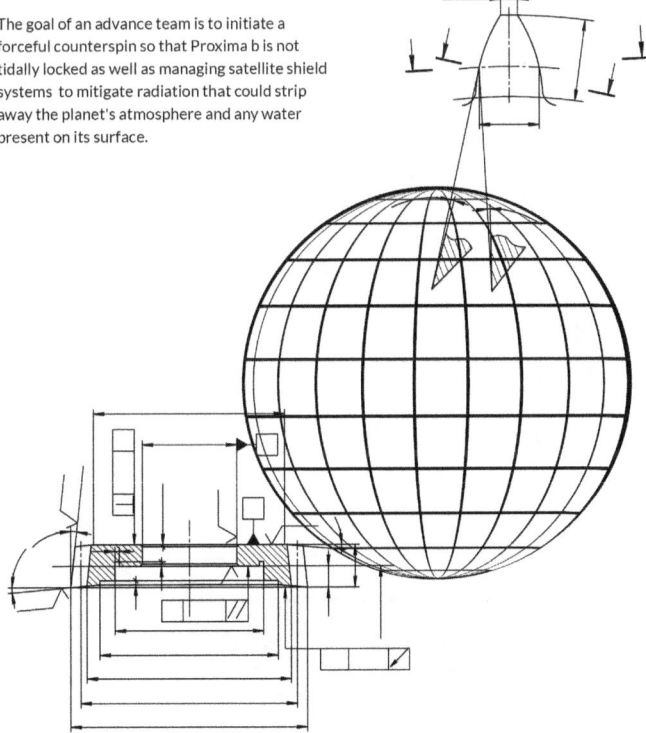